COCKTALES

VOLUME TWO

A collection of eight erotic stories

Edited by Miranda Forbes

Published by Xcite Books Ltd – 2012
ISBN 9781908766434

Copyright © Xcite Books 2012

Printed and bound by CPI Group (UK) Ltd, Croydon, CR0 4YY

Cover design by Sarah Davies

Contents

The Clearing
by Chris Ross

For Lucy, the temptation of an afternoon in the sun was just too much, so she grabbed a blanket, her iPod and some sun-oil and headed for the forest.

Joining the hidden path, she wound her way through the trees for about ten minutes, before leaving the path towards the clearing she knew so well. She soon arrived at the spot – a space roughly 50 metres square, surrounded by low trees and bushes and totally quiet and private.

She laid out her blanket on the soft grass, set out her iPod and removed her clothes, folding them for a pillow. Should I remove my panties? she wondered. She so loved to be naked in the sun. Looking around and listening, all she could make out was the sound of the birds, so she stripped her panties off too. The hot sun on her skin was making her slightly horny, as it always did.

Taking the oil, she put some into her hands and began to smooth it over her breasts, loving the sensations as she ran her hands over her sensitive nipples. Concentrating on one with each hand, she squeezed and gently tugged, feeling the tingling as they expanded and hardened under her fingers.

Lucy had always had sensitive nipples, but they were so often left neglected – something she could correct when she was by herself! She rubbed her fingers over them, slick with oil and warmed by the sun. She was in danger of getting carried away. Pulling her thoughts back, she moved on to her arms and shoulders, then on down towards her belly. Oiling her body always had an unfortunate effect on her. She moved down to oil her legs, but as she came up to her thighs she felt a familiar tingling sensation within her as her pussy began to moisten.

She looked around again. The clearing was empty as it usually was at this time; a gentle breeze blew across her skin and the sun blazed down. Who could it hurt? She was alone, wasn't she? She lay on her back, the soft grass beneath the blanket making a wonderful bed. As she parted her legs the warm sun on her pussy made her tremble slightly, but it was a wonderful sensation. She moved her hands across her inner thighs and gently brushed her outer lips with her fingertips. She slipped one inside and was not surprised to find how wet she was already.

Opening her legs wider, she slipped in a second finger, curling them inwards and upwards as she felt for her magic spot. A wave of pleasure coursed through her body as she found it and pressed gently, moving her fingertips rhythmically from side to side. She arched her back – something told her this wasn't going to take long.

Rubbing harder she felt the sensations begin, rippling up through her body as she caught her breath. She rubbed harder as the feelings grew more intense, her legs began to shake, her belly tightening, until suddenly she gasped, her fingers frozen, unable to move from the spot. She increased the pressure to prolong the sensation and held her breath.

As the orgasm subsided, she panted as she slowly removed her fingers and massaged them gently over her quivering pussy as she relaxed back onto the blanket exhausted. Putting on her earphones, she turned on her favourite music and began to doze.

Lucy realised she must have fallen asleep for some time, as the sun was now on the side of her face. She opened her eyes and was shocked to discover she was no longer alone! She quickly shut them again, but she didn't dare to move. Obviously, while she had slept someone had found the clearing and decided to stay. Carefully opening one eye again, she found herself looking at a man. He was wearing only a pair of loose shorts and he was sitting on a tree-stump with a small rucksack at his feet.

He was looking directly at her – and she remembered she was still completely naked. She knew he hadn't noticed she had woken up, because it wasn't her face he was looking at!

Still pretending to be asleep, she let herself sigh gently and moved a little which allowed her legs to part. The man quickly turned away but then let his gaze drift back, his hand moving to adjust the front of his shorts. She knew he must be finding this quite arousing – it was having the same effect on her.

Still feigning sleep, she moved again, and angled her body towards him. She wanted to allow him a better view. This time he didn't turn away. Through half-closed eyes, Lucy tried to look at him more closely. He was in his late 40s and he looked tall, fit and tanned. He had a full head of slightly greying hair and a light covering of chest hair.

She realised she found this stranger quite attractive and knew she wanted him to watch her – it was most definitely turning her on. She sighed again and let her hand drift down between her legs as she watched him swallow hard. She guessed his mouth had gone dry.

Lucy let her fingers slide over her pussy and she gently parted the lips. She was already wet again. She moved her other hand to join the first and opened her pussy to the sun, enjoying the feeling of its warmth on her inner lips, and knowing she was fully exposed. She moved her fingers to her clit and began massaging gently. She began to get lost in the moment, knowing all the time that she was being watched by a handsome stranger. She sighed again – her arousal was making her feel very brave. Not opening her eyes she said aloud, 'Please, won't you join me?' while she continued to play with her pussy and clit, and hoped she hadn't frightened him away.

She waited – enjoying the feeling of her fingers on her soft flesh.

She had heard nothing, but suddenly she felt a gentle kiss on her breast. She gasped, but knew he had taken up her generous offer. With his soft tongue he circled her nipple, taking it into his mouth as it hardened to his touch.

Oh, how she loved a man who gave her breasts the attention they craved. His hand found her belly and his fingertips lightly played on her skin. Lucy shivered, expectantly. His fingers moved further down to join her own, as he nibbled slightly on her now erect nipple causing that wonderful feeling of pleasure and pain. She felt a trickle of wetness escape her pussy and run slowly down between her bum cheeks.

Soon his kisses were moving down her front, pausing to tease her belly-button before continuing further. Without warning, his tongue was on her clitoris and in automatic response she lifted her hips towards him. His tongue licked and teased and probed, as his hands came up to roughly massage her breasts and engorged nipples. And then, abruptly, he was gone.

For a moment she felt lost and confused, and feared to

open her eyes. Then she sensed him again as he kneeled astride her head. His body now blocked the sun as he leaned forward to move her hands away from her pussy, his tongue running down her belly again before he buried his face between her legs. She knew exactly what she had to do.

She moved her hands up until she felt his thighs, then she slid them further upwards and inwards to find his erect penis hovering above her face. She opened her eyes to get a good look at his cock. She liked to see what she was going to get, so she admired the large organ that she now held in her hands.

She touched it with her tongue and felt his involuntary twitch. She circled her fingers around it, enjoying the stiffness she knew she had caused. Tilting her head back, she drew it down further towards her mouth and ran her tongue around the rim. Experience told her this could drive men wild, but somehow she felt that wouldn't be necessary in this case! But it was still fun.

She licked her way up to the end and let her lips close around the engorged head and began pulling it further into her. She slowly eased it back out again, all the time playing her tongue around it, until she felt his own tongue once more find her clitoris. At the same time he slid one of his fingers gently and slowly into her now soaking pussy.

She lifted her head, taking all of his impressive cock into her mouth until he nudged the back of her throat. Then she moved back again, intent on teasing him some more. Her hand gently squeezed his balls as she clamped her lips harder around his shaft, sliding him in and out. Concentrating then on the rim around the head of his penis she licked and sucked for all she was worth.

Meanwhile, he started to make gentle movements in

time with her own – penetrating her mouth, all the time letting his fingers and tongue tease her now aching pussy. Then his finger found her magic spot, rubbing firmly while his tongue flicked over her pouting clitoris. My God, she thought, how much more of this can I take?

As if in answer, she started to get the familiar feeling as her pussy began to throb and she knew she wouldn't hold out much longer. At that same moment, she felt him start to thrust harder at her mouth and knew his own moment had almost arrived.

Then she felt the first wave of her own orgasm grow. She thrust her hips off the ground and hard against his fingers, then threw back her head as the sensation tore through her. A burst of fluid exploded from her pussy as she experienced her first ever ejaculation. She slowly lowered her head and shoulders while she gasped for breath – and realised suddenly he was no longer on top of her.

Where did he go? thought Lucy and, more to the point, how does he *do* that?

She found out where he'd gone when she felt a pressure between her legs, gently forcing them apart and she understood there was more to come. He placed his hands under her bum, and raised her hips up towards him. He bent forward, running his tongue over her still-quivering pussy, darting it in and out of her hot pussy, before finally closing his lips around her tender clitoris and sucking gently.

Lucy moved her hands onto her breasts to tease her own nipples, rubbing and pulling, adding to the pleasure she was already feeling further down. Lowering her once more to the ground he inserted one, then two fingers into her, meeting almost no resistance – all the time massaging her clitoris with his tongue. He drew his fingers back, but then, as he pushed into her again, she felt her pussy being stretched a little.

Once more he withdrew and this time as he came back into her she felt the stretch rather more. She moaned softly and moved herself on his fingers, knowing that by now he must have all four inside her. Her pussy was now stretched to accommodate them, as she put her head back and sighed again at this new and unexpected sensation.

He continued to slide his fingers in and out, each time opening her a little wider, going a little deeper. She took a deep breath, arched her back, and tried to force herself onto him. But he followed her movements, teasing her and causing her to moan in frustration. Now she began to feel a greater pressure. Surely not? she thought, Surely this can't be happening?

But she could no longer help herself. Her passion had now taken over and she began to feel the adrenaline rush. She forced her legs wider apart as she drew her knees up, anticipating what was to happen, losing herself in the feeling of being stretched wider and wider, knowing that she was now gaping open for his inspection.

When it came, it took her breath away. She gasped as she took his whole hand into her. The sensation was something she could never have imagined in her wildest dreams. It was an intense pressure inside her that she had never experienced before.

She orgasmed instantly, her whole body shaking uncontrollably, her head spinning as she grabbed his wrist with one hand and forced herself onto him. With her other hand, her fingers found her clit and she rubbed it hard and fast. He slowly and carefully drew his hand out, before pushing it back in again and again, while her fingers were a blur on her clit. She squirmed and writhed against him, and then she threw her head back as the second orgasm exploded through her body. For a while she couldn't breathe. Then, with a huge gasp, she sank back into the blanket as he gently eased his hand out of her – kissing, licking and caressing her now gaping pussy.

Relaxing in the aftermath of this amazing new experience, she ran her fingers through his hair while he continued to lick and kiss between her legs and over her belly. Slowly he moved away a little, but instead of getting up, he rolled her onto her front and, putting some oil onto his hands, he began to massage her back. He was good at it too, easing her shoulders and applying a little pressure as he ran his thumbs down her spine. She began to relax with the combination of the heat and his touch.

Inevitably, his hands began to stray lower as he gently oiled her bum. She had always been proud of her curves, and he certainly seemed to appreciate them too. At first gently, then a little more forcefully, his thumbs strayed down into the crack between her cheeks, teasing her. Feeling relaxed and warm, she enjoyed the sensation as she had rarely received a massage, and certainly never in such surroundings.

Without even thinking, she raised her hips up towards him. In response, he knelt between her legs and, using her own juices, massaged her bum, straying between her legs and teasing her anus. She felt the unexpected tingle of yet another new sensation. He continued with the massage, but more and more his fingers teased her delicately. She reached back behind her to return the favour, and was pleasantly surprised to discover that his cock had recovered its former glory and was already standing to attention.

He eased closer and she let her fingers encircle it, rubbing slowly up and down. As she did so, she felt his fingertip push gently into her arse, causing the tingle to increase in intensity. Taking the lead this time, she eased her hips towards him, slowly drawing his cock towards her.

She felt him hesitate, and heard the rustle of a packet and realised what he was doing, but the waiting only made her more eager. She tilted her hips even more and, placing his cock in position, she guided him gently into her waiting pussy. In response he moved his finger further into her arse, causing her muscles to tense involuntarily, but she forced herself to relax. Today was a day for new experiences and she was keen to try everything.

She began to rock rhythmically against his cock and he matched the movements, withdrawing fully, before pushing in again, his hips hard up against her. She could feel the full length of him inside her as he continued to tease her other entrance. As his thrusts became more intense, she moved her own fingers back to her clit and began to rub. She forced her hips back harder with each thrust and she felt him add a second finger to the penetration of her arse. A little ripple of pleasure and excitement ran through her.

Never before had she felt the sensation of two penetrations at the same time. The feeling was surprisingly intense. She rubbed her clit harder as his thrusts became faster, his cock filling her as his fingers now began to thrust in and out too. All three sensations combined together, tipping her over the edge into an intense orgasm that made her cry out. Burying her face in the blanket, she clamped around his cock, as she felt his orgasm deep within her. He stayed still for only a few moments, panting slightly before withdrawing and slowly backing away.

She lowered herself down to the blanket utterly sated, buried her face in her clothes and, with the heat and exhaustion, she drifted off to sleep.

On waking, after what she was sure were only a few minutes, she found she was again alone in the clearing. She looked around, sure he must be there somewhere, but could see no sign, although her gently throbbing pussy, confirmed it had certainly been no dream. As she stood up and looked towards where she had first seen him, she saw something on the tree stump where he had been sitting.

Dressing quickly and collecting her things, she walked across to it. On the stump she found a single red rose of the most exquisite shape and colour. Beside it lay a small card, on which was simply written, To my beautiful forest angel, thank you! A small tear escaped her eye as she tried to remember the last time somebody had called her beautiful.

Though she returned to the clearing many times that summer, undressing and waiting, dozing on her blanket, the stranger never returned. But for ever in her dreams in that place, would come the amazing sensations of that incredible day. And the knowledge that somebody thought she was beautiful, gave her a new-found confidence to go out and face the world.

Cowgirl Honeymoon
by Tamsin Flowers

It was the fourth day of my fantastic honeymoon and I woke up as horny as a bitch on heat. I breathed in deeply to catch the intoxicating smell of my new husband and let a sigh escape my hungry lips. I slid across the bed to where he lay, naked and still in the depths of slumber, and traced the downy line of dark hair that swept down from his belly with my fingers ...

It had been my idea to come on a ranch holiday for our honeymoon; I'd dreamt of being a cowgirl since I was a little girl and the smell of horses and leather always turns me on to an extraordinary degree. Kyle had laughed when I suggested it but when I'd said I was serious, he'd shaken his head.

'No way, sugar. You'll never get me up on the back of a horse.'

He was adamant but I'd wheedled and whined for months in to the run-up to our wedding and finally he'd relented. We'd have five days on a ranch and then ten days on the beach. He was so in love with me that he'd agree to anything, so here we were at the Cougar Brook Ranch in Wyoming, staying in our own secluded log cabin deep in the woods. For the first couple of days I rode the horses and he rode me. I was in heaven – what girl wouldn't be, with a hot stallion between her thighs day and night? Then, on the third day I managed to get him into the saddle. It hadn't gone well. He hadn't wanted to enjoy it and he didn't stop moaning as we rode up a hilly track for the view from the top. And of course, when he fell off, he thought all his complaining had been justified and he limped back down to camp on foot, leaving me to deal with the horses. Last night had been the first night since the wedding that he hadn't wanted to screw me stupid.

Kyle grunted in his sleep. My hand had slipped down to his swollen cock. It was certainly awake, even if he wasn't. As it became harder, it pushed up into my grasp and I squeezed it playfully. It was big and beautiful and it was making my mouth water. I moved in closer and bent over him, gently running the tip of my tongue from the base up the shaft to the pulsating head. Kyle groaned. He was definitely awake now.

'Oh baby, work your magic,' he muttered.

I took his rock-hard piece deep into my mouth and started working on it with my teeth, my lips, and my tongue. I knew just how he liked it and his hips started to grind in response. His groaning became louder and more intense; he was shouting out as I sucked harder and harder.

Suddenly I felt his hands on either side of my head and he was pushing me away. I looked up, puzzled. He'd never asked me to stop before.

'What's the matter?'

'You gotta stop, sugar. I can't go on.'

'Babe, what's wrong?'

'I'm in agony. I can't move my hips. My ass is on fire. My back is killing me.'

I burst out laughing.

'You're saddle sore from yesterday!'

'That fucking horse. He bucked me off.'

'Well, if you hadn't yanked so hard on the reins ...' I muttered under my breath.

He pushed me to one side and pulled the sheet over his rapidly shrinking cock.

'I can't do it, darling. The pain's too much.'

I tried to hide my disappointment.

'I'll give you a massage,' I said.

'No, no. I've just got to lie here and wait for it to pass. I'm sorry.'

I sighed. The fires were stilling burning inside me and Kyle wasn't in any position to put them out. I got up from the bed and walked across to the window. The view of the mountains that surrounded us was spectacular and the sun was already high in the azure sky.

I wondered how bad it was or whether he was trying to punish me for getting my own way.

'Listen, sugar, I'm sorry to have ruined your last day on the ranch. But why don't you get everything packed, ready for an early start tomorrow morning? I'm sure I'll be fine by then.'

'On my last day? Are you kidding? I wanted to ride up to Autumn Ridge today.'

'Fine,' said Kyle. 'You go off and enjoy yourself. Don't worry about me.'

'But you'll be OK,' I said. 'A bit of bed rest and then I'll come and play doctors and nurses with you this evening.'

I leaned down to kiss him but he rolled away across the bed with his back to me and pretended to be going to sleep.

I stomped noisily to the bathroom and took a shower. If he was going to be like that, I'd be better off riding with one of the wranglers who worked on the ranch. He only had himself to blame, I thought as I roughly towelled myself dry. Then I pulled on my jeans, a plaid shirt and my boots and headed for the door.

An hour later I was perched on the back of a piebald Appaloosa called Mohawk, riding out of the ranch behind the quietly spoken wrangler who'd been assigned to look after me for the day. All I'd learned from our brief conversation before mounting up was that his name was Tex and that the enormous black stallion he rode was called Jet. It was hard to judge his age; his hair was bleached light blond by the sun and his skin was tanned and weathered – a real outdoors man. There were plenty of wrinkles round his sharp sapphire eyes from squinting into the sun but his body was toned and muscular and he mounted his horse in a single lithe move. I guessed he was in his early thirties and he looked much fitter than my younger, sports mad husband.

I'd asked him to take me up to Autumn Ridge and as he rode ahead he didn't bother with casual small talk. The strong and silent type. But I didn't mind. I rode quietly behind him, thinking out the details of what I was going to do to Kyle when I got back later on. That's the great thing about arguing with a lover – the making up afterwards. Mohawk's rolling gate tilted my hips backward and forward in the soft brown saddle and without realising it I was gently pressing my pussy against the hard leather pommel that rose up between my legs. It was meant for holding on to but as a warm sensation started to rise unmistakeably up my body I quickly guessed that the cowgirls found another use for it.

As we rode on through the dappled shade of a grove of aspen trees, I tried to keep my breathing under control so Tex wouldn't realise what was going on behind him. I had to be careful as he would glance back from time to time to check that I was still there and I didn't want him to catch me in the throes of silently pleasuring myself.

I took the reins in one hand and let the other one slide between my legs. I was thinking of how Kyle had taken me from behind on our wedding night with a passion so intense that we'd broken the treasured four-poster bed in the little country hotel we'd sneaked away to after the wedding. Through the thin fabric of my tight jeans I could feel the burning heat of my aching pussy and I was desperate to feel Kyle inside me once again.

Suddenly Mohawk stumbled and pitched sideways. My concentration had lapsed and before I knew it I slid out of the saddle and fell unceremoniously on to the stony ground. The breath was knocked out of me and for a few moments everything was confused blur of horses' legs, tree trunks and stones as I fought to get some air into my lungs. Seconds later Tex was at my side, then kneeling behind me and propping up my head on his bent leg.

'Just breathe slowly,' he said in his deep western drawl. 'You're gonna be OK in a minute.'

He stroked an auburn curl out of my face and then lifted up one of my limp hands.

'You got a nasty cut here,' he said and I realised that I had indeed gashed my hand as I fell. I closed my eyes. I didn't want to see the blood; it would make me feel even dizzier. I breathed deeply and things started gradually to return to normal. Tex sat me up and I could smell his musky scent as my head leaned back against his chest. I remembered what I'd been thinking about before the tumble but this time it was Tex who was pinning me to the edge of the imaginary bed. Shocked at myself, I sat up properly so I was no longer leaning against him.

'You OK?' he said, climbing to his feet. 'I just gotta take a look at old Mohawk here.'

I nodded, not ready to speak, and watched as he went over to where my horse stood, favouring one leg as he grazed the meadow grass beneath the trees. Although Tex had the same bow-legged walk as all of the cowboys, he carried himself in a way that told me he would be red hot between the sheets. I'd felt the hard muscle of his chest and the soft caress of his hands as he bandaged my cut. The fact that I was now breathing heavily had nothing to do with my fall. I had to face the fact. I wanted Tex and I wanted him badly – it was the first time I'd looked at another man since I'd met Kyle nearly two years ago.

I got gingerly to my feet and leaned against a tree. Tex was murmuring into Mohawk's ear and then he gently picked up the horse's leg and examined the hoof. He put it down and gave the beast a reassuring stroke along the flank; I wished desperately that it was my rump he was stroking like that and I had to bite my lip to control my ragged breathing. My heart was thumping in my chest as he came back toward me.

'Yup, he's lame all right,' said Tex. 'You'll have to come up on Jet with me. Mohawk won't be able to carry your weight.'

He tied Mohawk's reins to the back of Jet's saddle so the lame horse could follow us home. Then he gave me a leg up on to his own horse with an easy grin. I felt his eyes raking down my body as I swung my leg over and wriggled forward on the saddle to make room. Seconds later he was sitting snugly behind me, with the reins in his left hand and his right hand resting on his hip.

'Giddy up, Jet,' he said and I felt his thighs tightening against the horse's side.

I sat bolt upright, hardly daring to breathe and certainly not relaxing into the rhythm of Jet's stride. Although I was hardly touching him, I could feel the warm proximity of Tex's skin, despite the cotton of our checked shirts and the narrow space between us. It was at least a two-hour ride back to the ranch and I was already starting to feel turned on. How the hell was I going to survive the trek without making my feelings obvious?

But as I looked around, I realised we weren't going back the way we'd come.

'Where are we going?' I asked, swivelling in the saddle to look up at his chiselled features.

'Seeing as how old Mohawk is OK without a rider, I thought we'd carry on up to the Ridge,' he said. 'That OK with you?'

I swallowed.

'Sure,' I nodded, turning back to face forward.

But as we rode on in silence, I was finding it harder and harder to concentrate on the scenery. My back started aching from sitting so rigidly straight and the low, rhythmic sound of Tex breathing so close to my ear was driving me wild. I wriggled to try and get comfortable and my shoulder blades brushed up against his chest. That one move lit the fuse and, defeated, I slumped back against him and gave in to what I now knew to be inevitable.

'That's better, honey,' he whispered.

And as he adjusted his position in the saddle I could feel the burgeoning bulge in his groin pressing up against the small of my back, while my mons was rubbing up against the pommel with each swaying step. My breathing became faster and, completely without volition, I knew my hips were grinding back and forth against his.

His right hand snaked up my side and then popped open the front of my shirt. I wasn't wearing a bra and Tex growled with pleasure as his hand encountered my nipples, already proud and erect as they became engorged with longing. He twisted and pulled them between his finger and thumb until I cried out with the exquisite pain, then he leaned me sideways so he could bend his head around to kiss them. A pulsating electric current ran from my breasts to the pleasure centre between my legs and I writhed against him, moaning uncontrollably as he flicked his tongue against my nipples and gently teased them with his teeth.

As I begged for satisfaction, he dropped the reins across Jet's neck and used his other hand to start undoing the buttons of my jeans.

'Feels like you need this pretty bad,' he said as he slid his hand down into my panties.

I gasped. Within seconds his fingers had found my clit but then they searched further round, stretching deep into the warm, wet recess of my vagina. I quivered as his experienced hand explored and sought out my G-spot, applying gentle pressure with small circular movements. Then, with his thumb, he started to stimulate my clit at the same time. He had me slung across his lap and was literally playing me like an instrument – the sensations soared through me like music, building in a spectacular crescendo as I responded to his skilful touch.

As he worked his hand faster my pussy was awash with juices and flooded with pleasure. My back arched and my hips bucked as the orgasm ripped through me and I shuddered as he kept the waves crashing over me for what seemed like an eternity. It was like nothing I'd ever experienced with Kyle or with any other man. My soft moans had risen to cries of ecstasy and I was left panting and breathless. Holding me tight, he gently withdrew his fingers from my throbbing vagina and my body slumped against him like a limp rag. I was drenched with sweat and I could smell the earthy scent of my juices on his hand as he held my chin steady and bent to kiss me.

His tongue forced my lips apart and explored my mouth hungrily, and without breaking away from me, he slipped gently off the now stationary horse and pulled me down into his arms. I kissed him back; the monumental orgasm had hardly dulled my hunger and I could feel through his bulging jeans that Tex needed the sort of satisfaction that only I could give. I rubbed my hand over his crotch, pressing hard, and he responded with a low, throaty growl.

The ground was soft and moss-covered and we dropped to our knees in a small clearing of dappled shade. Tex ripped away my shirt and then his own while I battled with the huge brass buckle of his belt. As I got it undone, he pulled down my jeans and seconds later I lay spread-eagled before him in just my pale pink silk panties. He kicked off his cowboy boots and his jeans while I looked up, licking my lips and fondling my tits as I appreciated his spectacular physique. His rich, deep tan covered muscles that were sculpted to perfection but most breathtaking of all was the splendid cock that now stood free and proud, poised for action, above me. The skin was paler than the rest of him but dark veins throbbed along its astounding length and breadth. It was like a giant alabaster sculpture and I couldn't wait to feel it inside me. My pussy was aching for it and my hips angled upward as I splayed my legs, ready to receive my prize.

But Tex wasn't going to be hurried. He knelt in front of me and grasped the top of my panties with his strong hands. With a yank they were off and I saw his eyes light up as he tossed them away into the bushes. Then his head ducked down and the next thing I felt was the tip of his tongue gently exploring the soft territory between my thighs. With long sweeping strokes it massaged first the outer, then the inner lips of my vagina. It flicked softly in and out of the dark crevice and then I felt his whole mouth latch on to my clit as his tongue worked around it in small darting circles.

My back arched as waves of pleasure swept through me and then I added to Tex's efforts by putting my idle fingers to work on my nipples. I twisted them and pinched them until they were on fire and Tex's hands slid round to grasp my buttocks just as tightly, adding yet another level to the sensations coursing through my body. But I knew there was a part of Tex that needed attending to and I couldn't bear it a moment longer.

I put a hand on his shoulder and pushed him back until he was lying on the ground. Then with a quick twist I straddled him in the perfect sixty-nine position. His fantastic cock was now staring me in the face and I didn't waste a moment. I licked my lips and gave his throbbing head the tiniest of kisses. It jolted as if an electric current had been passed through it, and at the same time I felt Tex's tongue darting into my fanny, this time from a different angle. Then I opened my mouth, relaxed my jaw and took the whole enormous organ into my mouth. I started slowly moving up and down, using my tongue and my teeth to stimulate his shaft, while with my hand I squeezed his rock-hard balls until he moaned. It was as if we had created a circle of current that surged through our two naked bodies while we pleasured each other in the deserted clearing.

There was definitely some sort of primal sexual connection between us because at the very same moment we both chose to change position. It was time for the main event. I lay back on the moss, my hair a sweaty tangle around my shoulders and my body already flushed with arousal. My legs were slack and spread wide and I pushed my hips up to meet Tex as he powered down into me. His cock was far larger and far longer than I'd ever experienced and I could feel it deep inside me, pushing further and further as I arched my back toward him. He ploughed his way into me with deep, hard strokes and I wrapped my legs around his waist, pulling his body tightly against my own. His mouth dropped first to my right breast, then my left; the nipples were engorged and he sucked on them hard as they stood proudly to attention. Every thought left my mind as I surrendered to his complete control of my body and the sensations that seemed to be almost tearing me apart.

His thrusts became faster and faster and he pushed up on his arms, arching his own back so he could plunge deeper and deeper. As I reached an all-consuming orgasm, the muscles of my vagina contracted rhythmically and I could feel the hot fire of his come inside me. We both cried out as our bodies shook and shuddered with our own personal earthquake. Then he slumped down on top of me and kissed my neck so gently that I shivered with delight. His cock was still inside me but I could feel it softening as we both lay panting and glistening with sweat and juices.

The sun was sinking in the sky as we slowly got dressed in satisfied silence. Tex rounded up the two horses from where they'd been grazing, while I retrieved my panties from the bushes and tried to straighten my hair.

'You sure as hell know how to ride, cowgirl,' he said with a grin, as he helped me up on to Jet's saddle.

We never made it to Autumn Ridge but I was still able to tell Kyle it was a spectacular ride when I got back to our cabin. I know I should have felt guilty, and I suppose I did, a little bit. But he had been acting like a spoilt brat ...

He was still lying on the bed but he looked a bit chirpier than when I'd left him in the morning. He seemed to have got over his sulks; maybe it was the prospect of leaving for the beach tomorrow.

'I'm feeling much better, babe,' he said. 'Come over here, and I'll give you what you wanted earlier ...'

I looked across at him with a desolate expression.

'I don't think I can, hon,' I said. 'I'm sorry but I'm a bit too saddle sore myself after today's ride. You'll have to wait until tomorrow.'

Would You Like Fries with That?
by Sommer Marsden

Feel free to laugh if you must. I have a friend Charlene who will go on and on when drunk enough about how she loves a man in uniform. Charlene, being a friendly, fun-loving slut, means a Navy uniform, fatigues, police officer, fireman, EMT and the like. I will drink shoulder to shoulder with her, nod and agree. But what I mean by a man in uniform is entirely different.

It isn't much of an issue but for certain days when lunch break takes me out into the bustle and crunch of the city. *Then* it's an issue. I both look forward to and dread these days. I anticipate them wetly and warmly because I know I'm going to get off. I dread them because I know I'll probably end up gaining about a pound from the food.

Today it's McWilliams's. I slip into the warm, neon-lit clatter of the fast-food joint and suck in a breath full of grease and salt and fat. Heaven.

The lines are long. It's lunch time, after all. There are five raggedy lines and a crush of people. The staff look frazzled and overworked but one stands out. He's tall and lanky and barely legal. Definitely graduated because it's a school day and he's here, but not by much. This is probably his college money job and that makes me smile.

His shoulders are broad but still thin from youth, his face is peppered with light stubble and a shock of unruly dark hair pops out from under his regulation cap. I check him head to toe. McWilliams's striped uniform shirt – a white shirt with a navy blue pinstripe. Yellow tie with a tie tack shaped like a burger. A navy cap with the big McWilliams's logo. Dark navy pants, yellow belt and a smile.

I love a man in uniform.

I can't help but fidget with the hem of my dress as I wait in line. Each satisfied customer that passes, I get closer to my server. I can just imagine the starchy feel of his nifty shirt under my fingers as I get him naked. The tinkling jingle of his bright yellow belt complete with logo as I undo it. I shiver, rubbing my thighs together, listening to the subtly sultry whisper of my cable knit tights.

My boots clack over the bright red, not so clean restaurant floor and it's my turn.

'Welcome to McWilliams's,' he says. 'My name is Todd. May I take your order?'

Todd. His name is Todd and he is fabulous. White teeth and red lips. Blue eyes and smooth skin. He must not work the fryer. There isn't a single blemish on his beautiful face. 'Yes, I would like ...' Well hell. What would I like? I have no idea. 'An ... um, chicken sandwich, no condiments. A diet cola and ...' His lips are distracting me and I swallow hard. I can feel the annoyance radiating off the person behind me.

'Ma'am,' he says, exhausted already despite his young age. 'Would you like fries with that?'

'Um ... are they good?'

'For crying out loud!' The woman behind me barks and I turn to her, narrow my eyes.

'Oh, I'm sorry,' I say. 'I was under the impression that it was *my turn*.'

She is frazzled, obese and has three kids in tow. I turn

around quickly because I get the feeling she might want to do me bodily harm.

Todd leans in and my pussy twitches at that. Already under my pretty crème-coloured tights, my satin panties are wet in the crotch. My nerves are all jaunty and my skin is buzzing with anxiety and excitement. 'Miss, you really have to order. People tend to get a bit aggressive during the lunch rush,' he says.

'Oh, of course. I would. I would like fries with that.'

Todd nods and smiles. The smile goes straight to my cunt and then swiftly burns a trail from pelvis to nipples. I smile back. When I pay Todd, I slip him the note I brought with me. It's simple, really.

MEET ME IN THE PLAY COURT AT FIVE. I WANT YOU. WEAR YOUR UNIFORM. XOXO J

No phone number. Not even my whole name – Jamie – just orders to meet me if he wants to fuck. It's as simple as burgers, fries and shakes. I walk to the condiment counter and watch him open it. His eyes look up, he searches, finds me. Nod. He smiles again and it is all I can do to eat my chicken sandwich and hurry back to work. I lock myself in the small blue powder room, plant my boot on the toilet lid and push my hand into my panties.

It's Todd the counter boy in his stiff ugly uniform that I see when I rub slippery circles over my clit with my fingertips. I am kissing him, the bill of his McWilliams's hat brushing my forehead as I slide my other hand into my panties and push my fingers into my sopping cunt. I'm grabbing his tie while he fucks me as I get myself off two times, my pussy bunching eagerly around my juicy fingers as I thrust deep into my own body and I come.

I wash my hands, fix my face, and smooth my hair. The rest of the day is all business. My phone rings at three, it's Charlene. 'Meet me for a drink!' she commands. Her voice high and eager and bossy. She makes me laugh.

'I can later. I have to be somewhere at five, but I'm free after that.'

'Ooooh, fancy busy woman. That's fine! Where do you have to be?'

'I have a meeting,' I say and say my goodbyes. Maybe I'll tell her, maybe I won't. I kind of like having this little secret. This odd little thing that drives me sexually. That makes me fantasize and dream and wonder about what a man has under his ugly fast-food uniform. So far I have been with men from the fish and chips fast-food place, the taco place, the Greek place. Sometimes I like to think of it as an around the world with counter boys. No need to travel. I have a trophy from every stop.

'You look pleased,' Pat says from the doorway.

I start and then laugh. 'Oh, I am. Just having a good, good day,' I say and beam at him.

Pat has hit on me. I don't want him. Not now, anyway. He wears a grey tie and a black suit and wingtips every day. He also frowns a bit, worries and is rushed. I like my men a bit more young. And a bit more colourful in attire. And I like them to offer me a free refill or a baked pie when I order.

I snort, Pat frowns and I give him a finger wave. 'Sorry, back to work.' I shift in my office chair and feel the quiet moist thrill of a woman who has just gotten off and is anticipating doing it again. 'Come on five o'clock,' I breathe and try not to think about what his mouth will taste like.

It tastes like cherry soda and salty fries; his lips are sweet. He pushes me up against the deserted and defaced sliding board and slips his hands into my long brown hair. Such a

26

gentleman, grabbing hunks of hair instead of handfuls of ass. 'Here or in my van?' he asks.

I rear back, pleasantly more excited than I already was. 'You have a van?'

He nods, looking so pleased with himself I almost laugh out loud.

'Here?' I squeak.

'Yes, I do, J – what does J stand for?'

'Oh right, *I* do *not* have a nametag on, do I?' I ask, flicking his shiny gold badge with my finger. 'My name is Jamie. Nice to meet you,' I say.

He shakes the hand I offer but uses it to pull me in for another kiss. I run my hand up the gorgeously tented blue slacks he has on. I rub the head of his cock through too much fabric with my thumb and he stops kissing me for an instant, his lips still on mine, he just can't manage feeling all that and kissing at the same time. I smile against his soft mouth. 'I like that,' Todd says.

'My name or when I rub your cock like that?' I ask, doing it again.

'Yes,' Todd says and I laugh. He tugs me and my coat gapes open in the sudden wind like I might float away from him. A fairytale princess lifted from earth by gusts of silvery magical air. I squeal playfully and he tugs me harder. Then together we run and slip through the late winter slush to a horribly rusted green van with a small rear window shaped like a spade.

'Smooth,' I tease and he has the good humour to blush and laugh it off.

He opens the rear door and pulls me into the small square cocoon of not quite warmth. It's still chilly as hell but we're out of the wind. His hands are back in my hair, his lips are back on my lips, my fingers are plucking again at the gorgeous hard-on he's sporting.

I pull at his buckle and stop kissing him so I can hear the merry tinkle of the cheap gold fittings on his belt. His dick is long and smooth and so, so warm in my hand. When I squeeze him, he sighs in my ear like a long-time lover. 'Nice?'

'Nice,' Todd says. I can still taste salt on my lips from his kisses, so I dip my head to take the head of his cock into my mouth. His skin's salty taste rivals the fried treat he's eaten today. I suck and he bucks against my mouth gently. Still a gentleman. Still so sweet and nice. A nice young man in a nice shiny uniform with a nice big cock. This time *I* sigh and he pulls me up to kiss me, wrestling with the mess of my tights and my panties. My dress is shoved up, my underthings shoved down and Todd says, 'I wasn't expecting this today.'

'Does it happen other days?' I ask, but I lie back when he pushes me gently. I land in a bundle of blankets and jackets and some more uniforms if I'm not mistaken. My cunt clutches up at that. I wonder if I can beg, borrow or steal a whole shirt and not just some small token when all is said and done. But the thought flies right out of my head when he pushes his lips to my pussy.

'No. Not most days,' he chuckles and then seems to make it his life's mission to lick my clit until I beg. I fist my hands in a blanket and arch my hips up to meet him. He pushes me down with his big hands, he latches to my clitoris and sucks until bright yellow spots fire off behind my closed eyelids.

'You taste like sweet tea,' he laughs. 'Anyone ever told you that?'

I shake my head. No one's ever told me what I taste like period. 'Is that good?'

'Good? Jamie, girl, I could stay here all day.' I come in a long liquid shudder and he just keeps eating me, lapping at me with a tongue that possesses such a talent it has chased all the chill from the hollow, cavernous van.

'Oh, I don't know about all day.'

'All day,' he assures me, drinking me slowly now. Letting my body readjust and calm down and flicker its last bits of release through my pelvis. When my breathing stabilises, he pushes his blunt fingers into my cunt. One, two ... three. I gasp under him as if no one has ever, ever put their fingers in my pussy before. It's almost laughable but it is a new sensation. The intensity that he brings to what he is doing is staggering. And nice, if you really must know.

'I ...'

Todd looks up, tongue still gliding over my pussy lips, my clit, fingers still buried deep inside of me. My mind goes blank. I shrug. I have no idea what I was going to say. He's wiped all logical thought from my head. 'Will you come for me again, Jamie? You really have the sweetest juices,' he says and he grins. His grin is a mix of mischievous boy and the devil. I come for him. I come hard watching him eat me with his long eyelashes brushing his pale cheeks. His face is stunning – a work of art. When he shucks his pants and boxers, I realise that his cock is too.

'Wait,' I say, because he's coming at me and I know, I can tell by his face, that all he wants to do in the world is bury himself in me and fuck. And I want that too, but first ...' Come up here, please.' I whisper.

Out in the parking lot, people are laughing and yelling and dusk is falling because out of his tiny porthole window is the purple air of evening.

He comes up to me, putting his thighs on either side of my arms like I ask. He's basically pinning me that way on my back, arms soldier straight at my sides. His cock

29

slips between my breasts and Todd pushes them firmly together, forming tight cleavage to fuck. Every time he slides high between my tits I lick my tongue out and slide it along the weeping slit at the head of his cock.

He's lost somewhere, I can tell. His face almost shadowed, mesmerized as he watches his own cock slide up between the seam of my breasts and then takes in the sight of my red tongue darting out to meet him. His eyes are blue and wide when he looks at me and says bluntly, 'I'm going to come like a bottle rocket if we keep this up. It's too much.'

I laugh at his honesty. 'OK.'

I tug the shiny pearlescent snaps of his shirt and stroke them like good luck charms. My fingers tickle along the logo stitched on his pocket and I say, 'Ask me something fast foodie.'

Todd pauses but doesn't seem shocked or turned off. You'd be surprised at how often they get flustered and pissed. Instead, he spreads my legs wide and nudges my dripping slit with his cock. 'Um ... let's see, would you like fries with that, Miss?' He thrusts in before I can respond and all of my words fly off when he fills me. His cock has stretched me wide and my pussy is thumping with my pulse. I don't see myself making it long before I come again.

Where has Todd been all my life?

'I would. I would like fries with that.'

He's playing along and I adore him for it. He turns his cap around so that the back logo shows and I tug his tie though only his top button is done. He comes down with a crushing kiss and then nips my ear with his even white teeth. 'Do you need ketchup packets with your fries?' Todd flings my legs high on his shoulder, angles me, fucks me deeper so that I have to struggle to pull a single shuddering breath.

'Oh God, I do. I do need ketchup packets with my fries.'

Todd nods, his face set with concentration as he watches his dick slip into me and then tug free. Slip ... tug ... slip ... tug. 'Do you want relish?'

'I ... I hate relish,' I gasp. My cunt is growing tighter with each thrust. His fingers are so harsh on my skin I want to beg and scream and tell him to hold me tighter.

Instinctively he does. He grips my ankle in one hand, turns his head and nips my ankle with his teeth. 'Would you like a pie for dessert?'

The pain sings up my calf and I shake all over as the orgasm rips through me. He's thrusting hard and fast and his muscles are trembling like it's everything he has not to just come right that instant. 'I would. I would love a pie. I love pie. I looooooove piiiiiie!' I sing as every flicker and spasm dances through my pussy and I am grabbing his tie and possibly choking him to death.

Todd does not die. Todd pulls free, grabs my ass with both hands and turns me. The secretive sound of fabric being manoeuvred fills the van and then his golden tie drapes around my neck and I am ready to come all over again. 'My name is Todd and I'll be training you, trainee. First order is you must always be in uniform.'

He's rubbing the head of his cock to my pussy from behind and I'm holding my breath. When his hand snakes around and grabs the tail of the tie and slides it around so he can hold it behind my head like a rein, I moan.

Todd pushes into me slowly and then he tugs the tie like a leash. I feel my body grow tight and hot. I hang my head and inhale the smells of him. Young man, aftershave, fryer grease. He's fucking me and tugging that tie until his movements become fast and frenzied. 'You

31

will always be in uniform or there will be a reprimand,' he says.

He tries to sound authoritative. But he sounds like a young man about to shoot his load, but I am on the verge of coming again so I give him a hearty, breathy, 'Yes, sir. I understand, sir.' My fingers are pinching my slippery clit desperately.

'Good,' he says and gives my ass one firm smack. The smack does it for us both. No one is any more good. Todd comes with a roar. I sigh, my fingertips rubbing over my clit until I bear my weight on my forehead alone and come with him. Mine is much more quiet and exhausted.

We sit there in the dark van, breathing hard. Then Todd leans in and kisses me. It is a surprisingly tender, sweet kiss for a hook-up. 'I have something for you,' he says.

I hold my breath, hoping against hope and yes, he hands me a striped McWilliams's shirt. My very own. Not a badge or a hat or a tie or a key-ring. A *shirt*. That I can wear any time I want to remember this. 'Thank you,' I breathe. I kiss him again. I rather like kissing him.

'I don't expect to see you back, but you know where to find me if you want ...' he seems to consider his words. 'A refill,' he says, finally and grins.

I have never wanted a refill before. But I just might want one this time. Todd is not your average counter boy. I kiss him one more time, push my starched prize in my tote and run off into the cold darkness, my body still thumping and quivering like a cooling engine.

Under the Desk
by Charlotte Stein

The first time I do it, it's because of Steve Trebecki. Steve Trebecki, with his big, smooth hands and his distant smell of something sweet. Not to mention the swell of his perfect ass in those expensive-looking grey trousers of his. I'm pretty sure he always bends down right in front of the water cooler on purpose, just to get the pool of mostly women in their little egg-carton cubicles to look at him.

He wants people to look at his perfect ass, and sometimes I think he wants people to look when he comes in first thing in just bike shorts and some kind of super-tight work-out T-shirt, but mostly I just think: *I want to fuck you, Steve Trebecki*, while I masturbate at my desk.

It's all his fault – anyone could see that. He swans around, looking hot. What am I supposed to do? And yes, I know that most people retire graciously to the bathroom, and the cool comfort of a closed stall, but where's the thrill in that?

There's no thrill in masturbating behind a locked door – that's the truth. I want to do it here, only sheltered by the walls of my cubicle and the fact that most people are usually gone by the time I get worked up enough to do it. Hands in my knickers, legs just spread enough to get access. Nothing too fancy – just my middle finger pressed to my clit, rubbing and circling until I'm all wet and biting back moans.

The first time I did it, my orgasm was utterly electric. Not like any of the ridiculous, paltry things I'd felt before, while lying in bed with my vibrator or some man who barely knew what he was doing. No, that first in-the-office climax had bordered on painful, slickness soaking through my knickers and all the sounds I wanted to make pressing too hard against my squeezed together lips.

I remember going utterly rigid, feeling it all the way down to my toes and up to the ends of my hair. Face as hot as anything, body constricted in work clothes too heavy for it. Too smart for it. Too thick, too grey.

And that tie around my neck – God, why do I wear a tie?

Maybe because it feels even better, when I'm all boxed in. I'm closed off and buttoned up, but my hand is inside my knickers anyway and I'm rubbing and rubbing my swollen clit. It's always swollen now – hell, it gets that way the moment I start thinking of something mildly sexy, while at work.

I could think of drowning in oceans of come at home and nothing would happen. Not a twinge. But thinking about Steve Trebecki licking his lips, while at work ... yeah. I'm right on the edge, within seconds.

And it's not just Steve Trebecki. From him, I progress to all sorts of interesting things: surreptitious looks at dirty things on the internet, for example. All these sites I didn't know existed, filled with hard, rampant cocks and pouting, delicious mouths. In the beginning just the sight of an erection sets me off, but soon I'm wanting a little bit more. A greater thrill. Something dirtier, that someone could catch me looking at.

Like the video I find of a hard-bodied guy jerking himself to orgasm. Yeah, there's definitely something I like about that – a little mirroring, if you will, of my clandestine activities. He jerks himself, and I jerk myself. He comes – all of that lovely creamy liquid pouring over his still pumping fist and the thick stem of his cock – and I come too.

I think I actually make a sound for the first time, while watching him work his own spunk into his still-hard prick. Someone far away definitely asks me if I'm OK, and I'm pretty sure I manage a 'Yeah, sure, just a sneeze.'

Something like that.

And then there's just silence. Silence once again, in my boring little office. As though even an orgasmic gasp is nothing to get worked up about; why I'm fairly certain I could die and no one would bat an eyelash. I could gargle and choke and fall down onto the prickly blue carpet, and be found by the cleaning lady hours and hours later.

So it's not a surprise to me, really, that I get bolder. Who wouldn't get bolder, under these circumstances?

I go without knickers or a bra, and I sit at my desk just as breezy as you please, and after I've watched some guy frantically fucking another – instead of filing expense reports, like I'm supposed to – I pull my skirt up until I'm almost showing pubes. I spread my legs wide, and feel real office air on my slick pussy for the first time, and just as I hear Martin from accounts guffawing at something that dickhead Andy is saying, not three cubicles down from me, I slip one hand into the gap I've opened up in my shirt.

Now if anyone should stroll my way, lean over me to check that I'm not dead, they'll see a flushed girl with a hand inside her shirt, pulling and tugging at one of her stiff nipples.

And it is *really* stiff. I can hardly bear to touch it and, when I do, all of these fizzing tingles pour through me, searching out my clit with unerring accuracy. I'm pretty sure I could make myself come just like this, just with this worrying, twisting touch, but I'm also sure I want a little more than that.

I want to answer this guy I've started speaking to in some sex-chat room, while I fondle my pussy. Or at least, I want him to continue telling me what he'd like to do to me – me, the dirty girl who's told him she's masturbating while at work – as I do myself.

After all, I've only got so many free hands. For once, some guy can do all of the work while I make good use of my body, and touch myself all over, and wait for him to carry on talking.

And he does, bless him. He says that if he were lucky enough to catch me, if he found out that the neat little uptight girl in his office was really a secret masturbator, he'd take his cock out and make her suck it – right while everyone continued going about their business – as she carried on playing with herself.

He's got the right idea, I have to say. Not too rough about it, not too crude. Just nice and simple and direct, with lots of extra *Oh that's nice, baby, oh your mouth is so hot and wet. Suck me, you bad girl, finish me off with your tongue.*

Etcetera.

It really makes me wonder why I didn't try something like this before, because it completely puts it one step above simple masturbation, in the middle of a place where someone could catch you. Now I'm almost having sex where someone could catch me, listening to the lewd comments and instructions of another person while I gently slide one finger into my greedy, creaming sex.

He asks me if I'm going to come yet, and this time I want to answer badly enough that I take my hand out of my shirt, and type that I'm holding off. I'm avoiding my clit, so that this aching pleasure builds and builds and in all likelihood will make me shout out, when I finally let it crest.

To which he replies that he does the same thing, and one time waiting made him come so hard that it hit the underside of his desk.

And then I just start picturing this dirty little fucker, masturbating just like me in the shelter of his cubicle and beneath the shade of his desk, trying to catch all of the mess between his fingers and failing, miserably.

Then even filthier and more delightful – I imagine that it's one of the boring assholes I work with every day, typing away at someone he believes is just as dull. Maybe Steve, or Gregory, the boss. Maybe it's that temporary guy they hired, with the coal black hair and the sly face and the sharp electric blue eyes.

It could be anyone, anyone at all, writing the words: *I'm coming, fuck, fuck.* While I finally let my finger slide up and over my aching clit, circling it just once before I come, and come, and come.

This time he tells me that what he'd like to do is get me up on my desk, spread my legs and lick my dirty pussy. Those are the words he uses: dirty pussy. And he also says he'd like to make me moan and moan until everyone comes and looks, then just watches him lick my clit while he fucks me with three fingers.

Maybe cheering him on. Maybe not. Would you like that, Louisa?

I would, I tell him. I'd also like to give him a blowjob underneath the conference room table, while the boss gives us a presentation on synergy. Maybe I'd even slide a finger into his ass, rub his prostate while I sucked the head of his cock, waiting for him to be unable to take it.

He tells me I'm a dirty bitch; that much is true. I've found out all sorts of things I'd like to be dirty with since I started this whole escapade. I'd like to be dirty with handcuffs and blindfolds and other public places; I'd like to saddle some random guy and ride him like a cowboy.

Though that one's his idea, not mine. Apparently he enjoys being treated like an animal, right down to the carrot he'd enjoy me feeding him after I'm done galloping him around some not-so-private place.

Like the copy room. Like the conference room. Like the middle of Marks & Spencer.

In return, I tell him that I'd like to catch someone, *really* catch them, doing some naughty business somewhere public. He asks me where and my mind immediately goes to all my thoughts of the bathroom, and the rows of stalls, and how anyone could be doing anything in there at any given time.

But no, no. I don't want someplace so private. The doors are locked, it's *too* buttoned up. No – I want just a little bit more dirty and a much higher risk, like the stationery cupboard or the copy room, or at his desk, maybe. I could walk in or lean over him at his desk, and he'd stand up, flushed and embarrassed about the thing he knows he's been caught doing.

And then what? my mystery man asks me, but I'm not sure. Usually I come, before I get any further into the fantasy. Usually I can't decide what I want to happen next. Is he cross with me for creeping up on him, ready to dole out a punishment for my transgressions, ready to make me admit that I do the same thing?

But then mystery man types *No, no*, and I lean forward at my desk, avidly awaiting his next comment.

You're cross with him, he types. *What a disgusting little pervert he is!*

And my heart beats wildly, because I know he speaks the gospel according to my loins. Yes, yes. I want him to be a little pervert, just like me, and just like me he should be punished for doing such an awful thing.

Yes, he types, and there's something so grave and miraculous about that one word, bold and in black. Yes, yes, yes – you should punish him.

It's the only way he'll learn, he continues, after a long, long moment. *You have to show him the error of his ways, make him stand up so that anyone could see him, shove his trousers down to mid-thigh – just to prove to him how wrong he was.*

I understand almost exactly what he means. Once the bad thing is done, there's no sense in hiding it. Why try to cover up your shame now? The deed is done, the milk is spilt, and now you have to stand there with your cock out for everyone to see, still hard and probably aching and, oh God, I know how that feels.

I wish I knew how that feels. It's so much easier to be discreet when you don't have a penis.

Then what do I do? I ask, but he's way ahead of me. He's already laying it all out, in explicit detail.

Then, he says, *you parade me around the office.*

I can't help noticing that he's switched from "he" to "me". Not that I'm going to hold that against him.

I can hardly walk because my legs are shackled by my trousers. But I try, just for you. I try with my cheeks burning and my cock standing straight out and everyone laughing, laughing, laughing.

Using the word three times is admirable, I feel. Might as well paint the full jeering picture – maybe with people throwing things too! And him at the centre of it all, head bowed, face red, my fist clutching a handful of his shirt, between his shoulder blades.

I won't lie – I like that image. And I tell him that I like the idea of him doing the same to me.

I guess we'll have to trade, he types. *One week I get the abject humiliation, the next week, you. Skirt up around your waist, pussy all wet and bare – if you're not already shaved down there, I'd be only too happy to provide that service.*

Honestly, he's such a kindly sort.

And then, after I've paraded you around, I'd make you bend over my desk so that I could fuck you. Face in the keyboard of my computer, arse in the air, my thick cock between your slippery cheeks.

I ask him if he really is thick, just for clarification's sake, you know, and he replies that he's gripping himself now and it feels big enough to test the circle of his fingers. Which I have to say, I don't mind at all. Oh I like that, yes I do, and I reward him by typing that I'm just hovering on the edge of orgasm, one finger poised over my clit and barely touching, barely doing anything at all.

In response, he tells me that he's just moaned aloud – enough for anyone around him to hear. Though of course, nobody responds, just like they don't for me. I tell him that mostly they just say bless you, as though I sneezed, and he replies that he's going to have to make me louder then. He's going to have to tell me how slippery the tip of his cock is getting, and how close he is to going off, just so everyone can hear me whimpering with excitement.

Of course, whimpering doesn't really get me much. There's barely a whisper of papers moving or a sigh of attention, in response. But thankfully my mystery man has made me bold, so I press down hard on my aching clit, and cry out as though stung.

Are you making noise? he asks, and then even better: *because I'm sure I just heard you.*

Naturally I prickle all over, but I don't let it show. I don't stand up on tiptoe, straining to see over the cubicle walls for the bowed top of someone's head. I don't strain to hear him too – I mean, he's obviously just toying with me. How likely is it that he'd be a part of the same workplace as me, that we ran into each other just by chance in some random chatroom, and all the while he's been not ten feet away from me?

But either way, I thank him for his efforts at ramping up my arousal. He's good at what he does, and I appreciate the sentiment. My pussy appreciates it too and aches beneath my busily working fingers and all the thoughts of him being so close to me, rubbing at himself and fucking into his fist.

When I hear something like a sigh from far away and to the left somewhere, I almost come right there and then – even though I know it's not real. Other people don't really do stuff like this in the middle of an office. He's probably at home, hammering away one-handed at his keyboard, creaming himself over uptight businesswomen doing dirty things to themselves under their desks.

But when he says: *Did you hear that?* I won't deny a thrill goes through me. And it gets stronger as he goes on:

I heard you. In fact, I saw you, which is why I'm talking to you now. You didn't notice me, but I noticed you – with your hand inside your knickers and your teeth biting deep into your bottom lip. You were watching something called Horny Boys IV, *and you thought no one could see you. But I did. I watched you watching it, and just seeing the disgusting things that turned you on made me hard. All that cocksucking and dirty fucking and you all flushed and furtive, watching it.*

I went back to my desk right away, and jerked off in

your honour. What do you think of that, Louisa?

Only he doesn't say Louisa. He calls me by my real name. And I suppose I should be embarrassed or frightened or something else like that, but instead my entire body feels feverish and I type in little jerking stutters:

Tell me who you are.

For a long, long moment the cursor blinks and blinks, and no answer comes, and I think: there's no way he's going to tell me. This has all been some kind of tease, keeping me on the brink of agony or humiliation with my finger on my clit and orgasm just so close ... so close, but not allowed, when exposure and laughter are just around the corner.

But then he types two words, and I think of his sly, narrow face, and his electric blue eyes, and my climax wells up in me like something dragged from the bottom of a place deep and dark. It blooms in my clit and pushes outwards and upwards, past my lips before I can stop it and loud enough to make the shuffling of papers and the polite coughs very noisy indeed. Nobody acts as though I sneezed, not this time.

Except for him. The guy I hear as loud as a gong, above all of the humdrum sounds of the office. I hear him, going over as hard as I've just done and, when I finally come around, I laugh almost as loud as we moaned. Mainly because he's typed two words, in between fabulous orgasms:

Bless you.

42

All You Can Eat
by Josie Jordan

I scrape up the last of my chocolate mousse and sigh with happiness. 'That was amazing.'

Gary doesn't reply. He seems distracted.

'I love buffets,' I tell him. 'Actually, I might go back for seconds.'

But Gary's watching the people on the table in the corner, a young couple of around the same age as us. The girl has glossy black hair and a low-cut top. She *has* to be wearing a push-up bra. Nobody's boobs stick up that much on their own – not that men ever realise these things. It looks like she's berating her partner for something. He has his back to me, but he seems to be trying to calm her down.

'Nice looking couple,' says Gary.

And then I realise what he's getting at. Oh shit. He brings this up at regular intervals. Until now I've managed to avoid the issue, yet I've always feared there will come a point when I won't be able to.

In a desperate bid to distract him, I say, 'We should get another coffee at least. Might as well get our money's worth.' But I already know that it's not going to work.

'What do you reckon?' asks Gary, without taking his eyes from the girl.

Aren't I enough for him? I ask myself, and not for the first time. Of course Gary would say I'm missing the point. That we're young and it's "only a bit of fun." I've never dared to refuse outright, because if I did so, I'm pretty sure it would spell the end of our relationship.

Besides, if I'm honest, there *is* something sexy about the idea of it. Not that I can imagine myself ever actually doing it though. It's just a fantasy, that's all.

'They're going at it like an old married couple,' says Gary.

The girl raises her voice and I hear a snatch of what she's saying. '… forgot to bring a bloody tie …'

But she's drowned out by an aeroplane scraping up over the rooftops.

Gary chuckles. 'You can tell who's the boss in that relationship. So – what do you reckon, babe?'

'I'm not sure, Gary. Anyway, you can hardly just go up there and ask them.'

'Let's get talking to them and see what happens.'

Before I can stop him, he's striding towards their table. Not knowing what else to do, I reluctantly follow.

'Hi, guys,' he says. 'How's it going?'

Their heads turn. Others might not get away with such a direct approach, but Gary has the looks and confidence to pull it off.

The girl offers him a small smile. 'Not too bad. Yourself?'

'Mind if we join you?' asks Gary.

'Sure,' she says.

Gary sits down next to her. 'I'm Gary and this is Dawn.'

'Claudia,' says the girl.

'Hi,' I say, flushing furiously.

'I'm Adam,' says the guy.

I see him properly then, for the first time. He's totally gorgeous: tall and dark, with piercing blue eyes and broad

44

shoulders. I've always been a sucker for jeans and a classic white shirt, especially on a body like his.

I flush even more when he offers me his hand to shake. My own hand is damp with sweat, but there's no time for me to wipe it on my jeans. His palm is warm and calloused. I'm horrified to feel sparks as our skin meets. Quickly I retract my hand.

'You guys flying out early too?' asks Gary.

Claudia nods. 'We're off to a mate's wedding in Dublin. The flight leaves at six and we didn't fancy driving to the airport that early.'

'Our flight's at seven,' says Gary. 'We're off to Munich for a football match. Thought we'd chill out and get some beers in beforehand, but this place is dead.'

Claudia laughs. 'Airport hotels – they're all the same. You could be in New York, Paris or Shanghai and you'd never know.'

The pair of them continue moaning and I can't resist taking another sneaky look at Adam. His dark hair is cut very short and he's clean-shaven with a strong male jaw-line. As he toys with the teaspoon in his coffee, I notice he has the thickest fingers I've ever seen. I get a sudden mental image of one of those fingers pushing up inside me and promptly start choking.

Everyone turns to stare at me. Gary frowns. But I can't stop coughing. My saliva has all jammed in my throat.

'You all right?' asks Adam.

I nod, but I'm not.

Adam claps me around the back. His renewed touch flusters me even more, but at least now I can breathe again.

'Sorry,' I mutter, my cheeks burning.

'Can't take her anywhere,' says Gary with a nasty

laugh.

I stand up. 'I'm going to get another coffee. Does anyone else want one?'

'Nah,' says Claudia.

'Got one, thanks,' says Adam.

As I walk away, the inside of my knickers feels as wet as my palms.

When I return, Gary reveals that Adam and Claudia come from the same small town as he and I. I shoot him a nervous look. Imagine if we were to bump into them in our local supermarket!

But it's too late. Gary clears his throat. 'Me and Dawn have got an offer for you.'

I want to kill him. How dare he make it seem like my idea?

Adam and Claudia look at him curiously.

In a casual tone, Gary says, 'How about we swap partners for the night? Adam and Dawn. Me and Claudia.'

I brace myself, fully expecting Adam to lean across the table and punch him. Yet he doesn't. Instead he turns to see what Claudia makes of this.

She seems stunned. 'Wow,' she says. A quick glance in my direction. Then, '*Wow.*'

She looks at Gary with frank interest. I have to admit he's looking good tonight. He's wearing a designer shirt that I bought him for Christmas, and his floppy blond hair is carefully styled to make it look as though it hasn't been styled, if you know what I mean. With his wiry frame and brazen charm, he's almost the exact opposite of Adam.

I take rapid gulps of coffee, wanting to be anywhere but here.

'The swap would last for one night only, simple as that.' Gary smirks to himself. 'Just to clarify, it's a sort of all-you-can-eat deal until the morning.'

I can't believe he's just said that. The nerve of the guy! As if it isn't enough for him to have sex with Claudia just once!

Claudia and Adam look at each other again and I see something pass between them. I'm amazed that Adam seems so calm.

Claudia rocks back in her seat looking down at her fingernails, before flicking her gaze flirtatiously up at Gary. 'Deal,' she says.

'OK with you. Adam?' prompts Gary.

Adam glances in my direction. 'If it's OK with the ladies, it's OK with me.'

My stomach is burning up. I lurch to my feet. 'Just getting another coffee.'

Blindly I fumble for a clean cup. As I reach out to put it under the coffee dispenser, another hand and another cup do the same. Our cups chink and I pull back with an embarrassed laugh.

'After you,' says Adam.

'Thanks.'

I hold my cup under the gushing stream of coffee, conscious that he's standing very close. He's about six inches taller than me and his aftershave smells like an ocean breeze.

To hide my nerves, I say, 'My third cup. If it looks good and smells good, I keep coming back for more. These all-you-can-eat deals are dangerous.' Then I wish I hadn't said that. "All-you-can-eat" has acquired a more ominous meaning now.

'I know what you mean.' Adam lowers his voice. 'Look, Dawn, we don't have to do this.'

I freeze.

'I can tell your boyfriend's pushed you into it. We don't have to say anything, we'll just go upstairs and sleep, OK?'

To my shock, I feel a stab of disappointment.

Adam raises his eyebrows. A slow smile forms on his lips. 'You *do* want to.'

My expression must say it all.

His smile widens and I feel an intense rush of desire. Finally he drags his eyes from mine to fill his cup. In a low voice, he says, 'After all this coffee, I'll never be able to sleep.' He turns back to me with such a smouldering look that I sense a rush of heat to my crotch.

We walk back to the table. Gary is hard at it with Claudia, touching her arm repeatedly as he talks. I glance at Adam to see if he minds, but strangely he doesn't seem at all bothered.

'You ready then?' Gary asks Claudia as soon as Adam and I sit down.

I wince. *Ready for me?* That's what Gary's asking. He could be a little more subtle, but then that's Gary for you.

Claudia giggles. 'Your place or mine?'

Gary dangles his room key from his middle finger. 'Mine.'

'You got your key, Adam?' asks Claudia, getting to her feet.

Adam nods.

'See you in the morning,' calls Claudia over her shoulder as she and Gary leave.

Adam's eyes follow them until they're out of sight. He sips his coffee, looking thoughtful, and I wonder how he can possibly be OK with this.

It occurs to me that not long from now, Adam's cock is going to be inside me. My heart begins to beat very fast.

'So how long have you and Gary been together?'

Adam asks.

'Two years.' I don't want to talk about Gary, but I rack my brain for what else to say. Should we be discussing favourite positions? Should I tell him I adore having my tits sucked?

I feel light-headed. All I can think is that shortly we'll be fucking. I know Adam has said we don't have to, but I have no doubts about what's going to happen. We're going to bed together, and I simply can't wait.

As we sip our coffees in silence, it occurs to me that I'm not the only one struggling to get my head around this. Adam and I remain a careful couple of inches apart, neither of us knowing how to bridge the gap. I press my hands to my cup to hide the fact that they're shaking.

In a low voice, Adam says: 'So what do you like?'

'Sorry?'

His gaze rests on his coffee but he smiles faintly. 'What do you want me to do to you? Because I want you to enjoy this, you know.'

I gulp. 'I *will* enjoy it.'

'Come on,' he pleads.

I hesitate. Am I really about to tell a complete stranger what I want him to do to me? My throat closes up and I can't speak. Yet my gaze drifts to his fingers and Adam notices this.

'You want my fingers?'

Breathlessly, I nod.

'What else?'

It comes out in a rush. 'I want to wrap my legs round your waist as you fuck me.'

His eyes close briefly and now he's the one struggling to breathe.

A loud crash makes us jump. Behind us, staff are stacking chairs.

Adam frowns. 'Shit, are they closing already?'

'Looks like it. It *is* nearly midnight.'

'Is it? I drank way too much coffee.' A secret smile. 'I'll never sleep,' he warns again.

'Me neither,' I reply and our eyes meet.

I follow him to the lift, where he presses me up against the mirrored wall and kisses me passionately. His tongue pushes into my mouth and I suck on it, imagining that I'm sucking his cock.

We're both panting by the time the doors open at the eighth floor. He takes my hand and we race down the deserted corridor. After a brief fumble with the lock, we step inside a room identical to mine. I kick my heels off and the thick carpet seems to caress my bare soles.

Adam and I fall on each other. As our mouths lock, I slip my hands beneath his shirt. Up his smooth chest to his nipples and down to the inch of taut buttocks above his low-slung jeans. I feel his bulging erection through the denim as he presses himself against me.

Joined at the lip, we stagger towards the bed. Claudia's clothes are draped across it, but with one sweep, he brushes them to the floor. He lays me down and stands there before me. Slowly he starts unbuttoning his shirt.

There's a boyish quality to his face, yet he has the body of a man. His square shoulders and tanned torso suggest a lifetime spent outdoors. He doesn't belong here, in this bland hotel room. Then again, neither do I. Right now though, there's nowhere I'd rather be.

I peel off my top and he eases down my jeans. Now I'm lying there in my black lacy bra and knickers.

He gives a dazed grin. 'I can't believe this is happening.'

I smile back. 'Maybe we're dreaming.'

He trails a finger around the curve of my hip. 'Well if I am, it's the best bloody dream I ever had.'

It's nice to feel appreciated. I've put on a bit of weight lately and Gary never lets me forget about this.

Adam's eyes feast on my body. I grab him by the shoulders and flip him onto his back. Sitting astride him, I skim my fingernails down that hunky chest before unzipping his fly and tugging his jeans from his hips. In my haste I drag his boxer shorts down too and he laughs but doesn't stop me.

He's lying there erect beneath me, his thick cock resting against the dark hair of his lower belly. I reach behind to unclip my bra. Immediately, he pulls me down to take each of my breasts to his mouth, trying to cram in as much flesh as he can. I wrap my hands around his head, pulling him closer and moaning as he sucks my nipples.

Then he's kissing me again, his hot tongue exploring the insides of my mouth. His hand goes to my knickers. He cups the sodden gusset in his palm before hooking his index finger underneath the lace. I'm so wet that his finger slips straight inside. I bite down on his bottom lip. He responds by pushing his finger as deep as it will go and then sliding it out to be joined by a second finger.

'Is that what you wanted?' he whispers.

Speechless, I nod. I think I'm more turned on than I've ever been in my life. His eyes search my face as he makes slow circling movements around my clit.

'Got any condoms?' I manage to gasp.

'Not yet,' he says, tugging my knickers down. He stretches himself out alongside me and his fingers begin to work in earnest. He certainly knows what he's doing.

I wriggle with excitement. 'That feels amazing.'

'Just relax,' he whispers, leaning over to kiss me

softly.

He's using both hands now. Two fingers of one are thrusting inside; the fingers of the other are applying pressure just the right amount of pressure. The sensation becomes so pleasurable it almost hurts. I bunch my hands into fists. His large fingers maintain their steady rhythm. At a speed that astonishes me the waves of my orgasm arrive. And just as it does, he pushes his fingers as deep as they'll go, making my body leap up off the bed. He kisses me again as he eases his fingers out.

Still lying on my back, I beckon for him to sit over me. He climbs astride so that his cock juts out above my tits.

I raise my head and settle my lips onto the rosy tip. Enjoying my power, I make him wait there for a moment, his salt mingling with my saliva. Beneath my palm, I can feel his heart thumping.

Slowly I slide my mouth all the way down the length of him. He throws back his head and groans. Still throbbing from my orgasm, I reach down with one hand and start touching myself again. I suck his cock as deep into my throat as he will go, breathing in the clean soapy smell of his pubic hair. He groans more loudly, squeezing my tit to spur me on. I begin to pump my lips up and down.

Before long, he swears under his breath, catches me by the shoulders and presses me back to the bed. 'You'll make me come if you keep doing that.'

'I want you,' I say hoarsely.

He reaches down to take a foil packet from the suitcase lying open on the floor. As I watch him stuffing himself into the condom, I imagine how in a second he'll be stuffing himself into *me*.

He lowers himself over me. Yet now he's gone all

tender on me, covering my cheeks with tiny kisses. In my ear he whispers, 'If this is too fast for you, just tell me, OK?'

But I want him so badly I can barely think. 'Just get inside me, right now.'

With his strong fingers gripping his cock, he eases himself into me. Only the first couple of inches though, as if he thinks any more might hurt. He glances at my face to check my reaction. This guy has a really gentle side, but I don't want gentle just now.

Arching my back, I seize his buttocks and pull him into me. 'Oh God,' I breathe as his flesh sinks right the way inside. I lower my hips and thrust them up to his.

His hands clasp my ribs. 'Slow,' he warns.

But I wrap my legs around his waist like I imagined earlier. I'm bucking and writhing beneath him and then he loses it too.

His eyes flash as he pumps his cock in and out. I bring my knees to my tits to let him go deeper. He lifts my feet higher still, until my thighs rest on top of his shoulders. I slip my hand between our bodies and start touching myself again.

'Yeah,' he breathes. 'You touch yourself, baby.'

His thick beautiful cock plunges faster and faster; his balls slap my arse. I close my eyes, grinding my fingers into my pelvis and losing myself to the moment.

He slows. I open my eyes. 'I'm about to come,' he says in a strangled voice.

The thought of all that spunk about to fly out of him turns me on more than ever. I increase the speed of my fingers. With a strained expression, he slides his cock back into me, inch by inch.

'I'm getting close,' I tell him.

He creeps back out.

'Yeah, that's it, I'm almost there'

He presses back in.

'Yeah,' I gasp, 'Just fuck me, come on.'

He lets go, thrusting hard and deep. With a sharp inhalation, his handsome face screws up and his body spasms. As I imagine all the seed pumping out of him, my insides clench up and suddenly I'm gasping with a climax so intense that for a moment I fear I'm going to black out.

He releases my legs and remains inside me for a few more delicious seconds. Then, with a look of reluctance, he collapses to the bed. As we lie sweating on the smooth hotel sheets, I study his face. Is he thinking of his girlfriend? He must be. Yet he appears perfectly happy.

'How can you not mind?' I ask quietly.

'What do you mean?'

'You know. About Claudia. That she's ...' I can hardly bring myself to say it. I don't even want to think about what's taking place right now in a room not far from this one. But I have to face it. 'Fucking another guy,' I finish.

His expression is hard to read. 'None of my business,' he says.

'What?' I prop myself up on my elbow to stare at him.

'My big sis does what the hell she wants and there's nothing I can do to stop her.'

'Your ...'

Adam sees my face and grins. 'You thought ... Yeah, it did cross my mind that you two might have thought that. But I could see she was up for it and I didn't want to spoil things for her.'

I break into a smile. 'Shit. And here was I, wondering how on earth you could be OK with it.'

Adam's smile fades. He trails his finger gently across

my face. 'What about you though? You weren't really into this, were you?'

'I wasn't at first,' I admit. If I've learnt one thing from the past hour, it's how good it feels to be with a guy who actually cares about me. I swallow. 'I guess I'm beginning to realise Gary isn't the right person for me.'

Adam raises his eyebrows. 'So how about I give you my number then?'

Wow. That certainly softens the blow. I lower my head to kiss him again, thinking of all the things I still want to do to him. 'I might just take you up on that. In the meantime, remember what I told you earlier?'

'What?'

I smile down at him. 'If it looks good and smells good, I keep coming back for more. This is all-you-can-eat, don't forget. Do you think you can handle that?'

Adam guides my hand down to his rapidly stiffening cock.

One Item or Fewer
by Elizabeth Coldwell

The dress hangs in front of the wardrobe, whisper thin. You watched me hold it up to my body earlier, imagining how it would look when I put it on. 'You'll be able to see everything,' you said, but the lustful tone in your voice made it clear that's not a bad thing. After all, the point of tonight is to be daring in a way I never have before.

I've been looking forward to Rob's party ever since we received the invitation. It's become an annual institution, every Midsummer's Night without fail. Rob is one of those unfortunate people whose birthday falls in the week between Christmas and New Year, so tends to get lost in the wider celebrations. When he was a kid, his parents used to compensate by throwing him a special summer party. It's a tradition he revived as soon as he moved into the house he owns now, with its big, high-ceilinged rooms and sprawling garden.

And this won't be any old party. There's always a theme, a dress code to be followed. There have been some memorable ones over the years: *Vampires And Virgins*, *Roaring Twenties*, *At The Bottom Of The Sea*. Everyone competes to see who can wear the best costume, but it's always been noticeable how many of the women take it as an excuse to wear an outfit that's as revealing as they can possibly get away with. I swear if the theme was *Night Of The Living Dead*, Rob's house would be crawling with slutty zombies. So this year, now his divorce is final and he's off the leash at last, he's taken their exhibitionistic tendencies to their natural conclusion, by making this a "one garment only" party.

I emerge from the bathroom freshly showered, wrapped in a fluffy bath sheet that conceals far more of me than the dress will tonight. As I smooth body butter into my legs and blow-dry my hair to a tousled bedhead, I keep casting glimpses at the indecent little outfit, wondering if I'll really have the courage to wear it. If I don't, it'll be a waste of an afternoon spent carefully removing the outer lace sheath from the taupe satin interior. With that lining, the dress was pretty but safe. Without it ...

'Taxi'll be here in ten minutes, Honor,' you remind me. It's OK for you. You've been dressed and ready for ages; your one garment a favourite pair of baggy blue beach shorts. They show off your nicely muscular thighs and a belly that's as flat as it was the day we met, ten years ago, but they hardly drag you out of your comfort zone. Still, tonight's about me, not you. We both know that. If everything goes to plan, tonight will be the night you finally share me with another man.

I usher you out of the room so I can finish getting ready in peace. Taking a deep breath, I drop the towel and step into my dress. It zips up with a soft rasp, and I risk a glance at my reflection. As we'd hoped, the loose floral pattern of the lace hides nothing. My nipples are visible, already beginning to pucker with the excitement of seeing myself so scantily clad. So is the fluff of pubic hair I've trimmed down to a triangle so small it may as well not be there at all. If you were here, now, instead of waiting patiently downstairs, I know you'd be tempted to just forget about the party and fuck me where I stand. Not that

I'd object, but I need other people to see me like this. I need Rob to see me.

A horn hoots in the street outside. The taxi is early, and I slip on my coat before grabbing my bag. No sneaky preview for you before we get to the party.

If the driver wonders why my coat is buttoned to the neck on such an unseasonably sultry June night, he doesn't say anything. You've thrown on a hooded sweat top, still Mr Casual as we slide into the back seat together. Your hand is itching to slide up beneath the coat, to take advantage of my knickerless state, but I thwart you by linking my fingers with yours.

'Not yet, darling,' I whisper tenderly in your ear as the taxi pulls away from the kerb. 'It'll be worth the wait, trust me.'

There's hardly any traffic parked on the quiet lane where Rob lives. I can't work out if that means we're among the first to arrive or if, like us, the other guests are choosing to take taxis so they can enjoy a couple of glasses of Rob's deliciously potent punch without the fear of being over the limit.

Rob greets us at the door, beaming broadly. He's dressed more conservatively than I'd expected, in a pair of shorts that are no shorter and no tighter than yours, but he looks good. Positively edible, in fact. The sun has bleached white-blond spikes in his fair hair, and his lean, compact body is lightly tanned. His garden is so secluded, so perfect for sunbathing naked, I can't help wondering whether there is white flesh beneath those shorts or if every last inch of him is that same enticing shade of honey.

'Owen, Honor, great to see you.' He accepts the bottle of Australian Shiraz you hand him with a nod of appreciation. 'You can leave your coats and shoes in the closet by the downstairs loo, then come through to the garden. I'm serving drinks out there.'

When I shrug the coat off my shoulders, your mouth gapes open like a landed fish. Your eyes seem to burn into my hardly concealed tits. Those shorts of yours give little away, but I'm sure you're stiffening inside them.

Grabbing me in a hug that tells me everything I need to know about the state of your cock, you murmur, 'You look fucking amazing.'

'Do you think Rob's going to like it?' I ask.

'Honor, he looks at you like he wants to jump your bones when you're in a sweater and jeans. Dressed like that ...' You don't need to say any more. The feel of your hard-on is giving me all the reassurance I need.

Walking out into the garden, we're greeted with the sight of a dozen or so of Rob's friends and colleagues, as close to naked as we have ever seen them. A couple of the guys have had fun with the dress code. One of Rob's football-playing mates has come in a wetsuit. Another is in a pale pink all-in-one that, coupled with his shaven head, has the effect of making him look like an oversized baby.

Everyone else seems to be taking it more seriously, though I'm not quite sure what category the man in the Borat-style lime green mankini falls into. The strips of Lycra that comprise his costume reveal a surprisingly hairy body, with thick black tufts sprouting on his chest, back and shoulders. There's even a darkish, peachy fuzz on his admittedly spectacular arse. I have to admire his confidence in carrying off such an unbelievably skimpy costume, but my fantasies have never leaned towards men who come complete with their own fur coat.

Several of the women are in lingerie, mostly pretty teddies and full-length slips, though one girl from Rob's old office, who's always loved showing off her body whatever the theme might be, wears only a pair of ruffled pink stripper knickers. The ties on the side beg to be undone, and I'm sure that once the booze really starts to flow, she'll end up as naked as she's no doubt hoping.

Another couple, who always make a point of coordinating what they wear, are in plain black T-shirts, which finish only an inch or so below crotch level. What, in other circumstances, would be one of the most boring things you can wear is completely subverted by the fact they're both bare beneath those T-shirts. One careless movement and her pussy, his cock, will be exposed to anyone who might be looking. And I'm looking, particularly as his T-shirt appears to be tented slightly at the front by the beginnings of a healthy erection.

While I'm being distracted by all the flesh so blatantly on display, you're striding towards the table where Rob has set out the drinks. A woman I recognise as Rob's former boss, a no-nonsense Yorkshire lass made good, raises her drink in greeting as I follow behind you. Her outfit of choice is a stunning silver mink coat – fake, I assume, though I don't doubt she could afford the real thing if she chose.

She catches me eyeing her. 'Well, people are always saying I'm all fur coat and no knickers, so I thought I'd prove it.'

'Bet you wish you'd worn something a little cooler,' you say.

Her laugh is forged from pure nicotine. 'Don't worry, love. If I get too hot, this is coming right off.'

That's when I realise this party is a couple of glasses of punch away from becoming a full-blown orgy. The girl in the stripper knickers has a pierced nipple, I can't help but notice, the silver barbell that adorns it glittering in the evening sun. Normally, I wouldn't consider another woman in a sexual way, but my mind drifts to what it might be like to take that nipple in my mouth, feeling the barbell cold against my tongue...

'Penny for them,' a voice says, as a glass of something red and fruity, topped with a paper umbrella, is pressed into my hand. I take a sip, tasting rum and plenty of it.

'Oh, I was just taking in the view,' I reply, turning to face Rob. 'You've outdone yourself with this punch, by the way.'

'Oh, it's just a little something of my own invention. I call it Wild And Willing.'

'Which pretty much sums up everyone here.' I'm aware of you, watching me from two feet away, silently giving me your permission to be as flirty with Rob as I want.

'Yeah, they've really embraced the theme of the party. As, I'm pleased to see, have you.' His tone grows lower, more conspiratorial. 'Your tits look fantastic in that dress.'

The words have my cunt twitching with lust, and if I pushed my fingers between my legs I know they'd come away wet. I've wanted Rob for so long, and tonight you're going to let me have him. I feel light headed and giddy, and it has nothing to do with the punch.

Behind us, there's a sudden squeal, answered by a burst of laughter. It alerts us to the fact the girl with the pierced nipple is no longer wearing her elaborate knickers. A bloke in tiny yellow Speedos that leave nothing to the imagination is waving them above his head, while the Borat-alike and a couple of his friends cheer him on. She's making a half-hearted attempt to grab them back, but it's obvious she's loving the fact everyone can now see her cleanly shaved pussy.

'Good job you've got no neighbours,' you comment to Rob. 'Can I top up your punch, Honor?'

I look at my glass, realise I've almost drained it without noticing. You take it from me, giving me the excuse to be alone with Rob just a moment longer. It feels like we're standing in the still eye of a hurricane, while the madness rages around us. Even so, I want to be somewhere else. Somewhere private, where I can act on the ever-deepening need I have to see Rob stripped of those baggy shorts.

You must be reading my mind, because when you return with our drinks, you utter the words that are guaranteed to raise the stakes. 'Rob, you know I wouldn't mind if you fucked Honor.'

Rob's face is a picture as he tries to work out if he's heard you correctly.

You pull me to you with your free hand, stroking my nipple with your thumb almost absent-mindedly. 'She's all yours if you want her. All I ask is that I'm there to join in.'

'Are you OK with this?' Rob asks me, as though alarmed by my silence on the matter.

Truth is, I haven't been able to say anything, because I'm so churned up with giddy anticipation. Inside, though, I'm screaming at you to say yes. Somehow I manage to find my voice.

'I want this. We want this. What do you say, Rob?'

'Well, I shouldn't really leave my guests unattended ...' As we glance round, we see that Mr Speedos is now kissing the girl he stripped of her knickers, his hands kneading the cheeks of her arse as she grinds herself on to his swimwear-clad bulge.

'I think they can manage without us,' you comment, in a tone as dry as the Sahara.

'Let's go inside,' Rob says. As we walk up the path towards the house, you holding one of my hands, Rob holding the other, no one pays us the slightest attention. Perhaps our disappearance will be their cue to unleash the pent-up lust that hovers just beneath the surface of this gathering, pair off and fuck on the lawn.

I've been in Rob's house so many times, but I don't think I've ever seen the inside of his bedroom. It's a single man's room, all right; the bed's king-sized but the duvet is rumpled, the pillows scattered everywhere. There's a portable TV with a built-in DVD player on top of the chest of drawers, angled so he'll be able to watch it in bed. Prominently on the top of the pile of DVDs beside it is a box featuring a busty model dressed as a schoolgirl and licking a lollipop, her nipples hard and prominent through the shirt knotted beneath her midriff. A vision flashes into my mind: Rob, propped up against the pillows, slowly stroking his cock as, on screen, the girl in the porno has her tight white knickers pulled down and her arse soundly spanked.

Rob spots what I'm looking at, and flashes me an unrepentant grin. The vision changes, and now it's my arse he's spanking. The thought gets me hot and bothered all over again, but I'm still not sure how we're going to kick this little threesome off.

That's when you take control. 'Go on, Rob. Strip her.'

Given that I'm almost naked as it is, all Rob has to do is tug down the zip. The grating as the teeth are pulled apart seems crazily loud and I realise we're all holding our breath, aware of the growing tension in the room. I step out of the skimpy lace sheath. Rob pulls me into his arms and we kiss. His mouth tastes of rum punch and his lips are surprisingly soft.

We collapse on to the bed, mouths still mashed

together. At your urging, I free his cock from his shorts, and stroke the fat, veined length of it. Somehow your hand works its way between my legs, finding my slick pussy. You're determined not to be a passive spectator. Instead, you're directing us to move into a position that gives you easier access to my clit. Happy to oblige, I kneel up, giving you a perfect view of my sex lips as they pout at you. Your finger traces teasingly along them, and I almost lose my grip on Rob's cock

'Nice and juicy,' you murmur. 'Perfect for fucking.'

I know you want to watch Rob screw me first, and by now I'm more than ready to have that gorgeous tool inside me.

You fish for something in the pocket of your shorts, tossing it to Rob. 'Time to rubber up, mate.'

He rolls the condom down on to his erection. Considerate as ever, you've made sure the latex is ribbed – for my pleasure. Not that you're not loving what's happening too. Though I can't even begin to know what's going on inside your head, at the moment where your most cherished fantasy is finally about to be brought to panting, sweating life.

Poising myself over Rob's groin, I guide his cock into place and sink down. So used to your dimensions, it takes me a moment to adjust to his extra girth. Catching sight of myself in his mirrored wardrobe door, I almost laugh at the wide-eyed surprise on my face.

As I feel him sliding slowly into me, I look over at you. Your shorts are off and you're stroking yourself deliberately. You give me a wide smile of love and gratitude, and I can't help returning it. How many years has it been since I've had sex with anyone other than you? It certainly hasn't grown boring in all that time, but now the strangeness is wearing off, I'm relishing having another man inside me.

Sounds drift in through the open window, laughter and what could be a man's deep grunting, and I wonder what's happening down in the garden. It's only a brief distraction. Rob is reaching up to grab my tits, pinching my nipples roughly. Fired up by his caresses, I grind down hard, matching his ferocity with my own. With a despairing groan, Rob's body stiffens beneath me, and he hangs on to my hips, keeping me still as he comes.

He pulls out, flopping on his side on the bed as you take his place. You urge me up on my hands and knees, wanting to take me from behind. Easing your way into my depths, you hold steady for a moment. Your voice is an excited growl in my ear. 'I can tell he's stretched you just a little. Did it feel good?'

'It felt absolutely brilliant,' I reply sincerely. 'But so do you.'

It's no word of a lie. Without the impediment of a condom – the privilege all those years of monogamy affords you – your cock is hot and vital inside me. You thrust into me with hard, fast strokes. Rob reaches over and toys with my hanging breasts, then turns his attention to my clit, rolling it between his fingers.

You make a strange, strangled noise in your throat, and when I check our reflection, I realise that as Rob is playing with me, the heel of his palm keeps catching your balls. The movement can't be anything but deliberate, and from the look on your face it's not unpleasant, either. Seems I hadn't considered all the possibilities when two men and a woman start to have fun together. Maybe I should start giving them some serious thought.

But thinking seriously about anything is getting harder, given the combination of Rob's finger work and your remorselessly thrusting cock. Seems like having you work on me in tandem has wound every nerve, every fibre in my body as taut as it has ever been. Just when I think I can't take a moment more of this delicious torment, you shift the pace of your stroking up a gear. That's all it takes for the pleasure coursing through me to reach critical mass. My pussy muscles clench round your shaft as I come harder than I think I ever have, wringing your orgasm from you in the process. Face contorted in ecstasy, the cords in your neck standing out, your bullish roar is so loud they must be able to hear it out in the garden. Not that I care. Slumping into a tangled pile of limbs with you and Rob, everything that matters at this moment is right here.

'So how was it?' you ask eventually.

'Wonderful,' I reply, taking the time to kiss each of you in turn. There's so much more I want to add. How this evening has surpassed anything I could have dreamed of. How I wish we'd had the courage to try this ages ago, and how much I want to try sucking your cock while Rob fucks me. Or – and this thought really intrigues me – watch him suck your cock, instructing him to take you deep into his throat. Instead, forcing myself to think about what might be happening down on the lawn, I ask, 'Don't we have a party to get back to?'

In synchrony, the two of you shake your heads. Then Rob, making it perfectly clear where he'd rather be, slithers down my body to lick the last oozing remnants of your come from my pussy, and our own private party begins all over again, with not even one garment to impede our fun.

Star-fucker
by Jade Taylor

I never was a star-fucker.

There were too many about in this business, too many bothered about their hair and their clothes, who they were photographing and whether they could fuck them, rather than the composition, the *art*.

But that was never me. You started thinking like that and your work suffered; you weren't considered a professional any more once you stopped being the one taking the photos and became the one in the photos, dressed in revealing outfits in the Sunday tabloids with Max Clifford on speed dial.

But kissing and telling had never been my thing.

Not that I ever had anybody famous to kiss and tell about; that just wasn't me.

That's partly why I got the job: discretion. I wouldn't sell out whomever I was photographing so that the paparazzi could gather outside like vultures looking for the dead. Whomever I photographed was between them, the camera and me.

Another was that I was getting good. Still young enough that I was finding my style, still brave enough to experiment, my commissions regularly coming from the edgier magazines.

And last, but not least, I seemed plain. I never saw the sense in dressing up for work, no make-up and flat shoes seeming much more practical, and nice clothes only getting ruined by the chemicals I use. Dressing up and fucking was for the weekend, and God knows I could find enough boys to play with *without* compromising my reputation.

So it was me, the anti-star-fucker, who the editor called.

But for every rule there's an exception, and he was mine.

I couldn't tell her that it was different this time; that there was one star I'd love to fuck.

Sure, we all knew his reputation, the bragging about how much he could drink and the women he'd bedded – no doubt she thought I was level-headed enough to take it all in my stride, brush him off like other women seemed unable to. Or maybe she thought he wouldn't want me in my flat shoes and thick-rimmed glasses, appearance screaming not to touch.

But she'd never seen me glammed up.

She didn't know that when I wasn't in my dark-room I was at the gym, that while baggy T-shirts and many-pocketed combats were ideal work-wear, I preferred a sexy dress and high heels away from my job.

She didn't know that I was mad about him, that I'd been fantasising about him for as long as I could remember.

You could keep all the other mega-stars; the vain actors more bothered about being photographed from the "right" side than the person behind the camera, the action heroes who wore more make-up than I did, the sexy singers so full of angst they had no room for anything else; they did nothing for me.

But he was different.

I'd first seen him in some crappy daytime soap, his

acting appalling but with looks you couldn't ignore; tall and dark-haired with those puppy dog eyes making you unsure whether you wanted to mother him or fuck him first. The broad shoulders, the narrow waist, that tight, tight bottom.

It didn't hurt that the soap required scenes of him stripping almost daily.

Back then it was a teenage crush, adolescent hormones looking for the likeliest target, our worlds never likely to meet. I was the girl in braces who found it easier to hide in a darkroom than talk to boys, back then a hobby that meant bullying rather than encouragement.

His acting got better and he moved to prime-time TV – fewer scenes with unnecessary stripping and more magazine interviews with glossy photo spreads. Then he moved to Hollywood, somehow bypassing the "best friend who gets killed" roles and straight to the romantic lead, those smouldering eyes finally put to better use.

And now *I* was to take those photos that would promote his latest film.

I couldn't stop thinking about him.

Every night as I lay in my bed my hand went between my legs, and instead of planning what photos I would take, of how to make mine different from the rest, I plan what I want to do to him.

The photos of him these days are all glossily seductive, him dressed in a smart suit, sexy but sophisticated, suave and handsome.

That's not what I want.

I want the raw sexiness that all his admirers know is there underneath the gloss, the cheekiness that's so appealing laid bare. I want it to be blatantly obvious in my photos.

I'm not sure if this is what my editor wants. The rack of beautifully cut suits she has sent over to my studio suggests not, but I know that she trusts my talent, that though I'm almost obsessed by the thought of having him, I'm not blinded by lust; that this will work.

I get a bed moved in to my studio, the difficulty of doing so more than outweighed by the thought of him in it. I make it up with crisp white sheets, knowing how good his olive skin will look against it. I lie in it touching myself, imagining him lying naked beside me, wishing my hands were his.

He walks in with his entourage like he owns the place, not even deigning to introduce his people as they spread out around my work area, taking over like locusts, too busy fiddling with his phone to say a word to me.

'And these are?' I ask, gesturing around the room.

'Hair, make-up, publicist, assistant, stylist,' he says in an off-hand way, still doing something on his phone, as if everyone should expect to walk around with such people, and he's so blasé that however attractive he may be, I'm already furious with him.

'Aren't you big enough to do this on your own?' I ask, stepping closer to get into his space, determined to get his attention. He might be used to women being in his personal space, but he's more used to them fawning over him, not getting ready to blow a fuse.

His eyes meet mine for the first time, and he smiles, that lazy million dollar smile that's made him famous throughout the world.

I don't smile back.

He holds it for a minute, waiting for me to cave, but I don't; he's fucking gorgeous but I'm fucking stubborn.

He steps back and stops smiling.

'Okay gang, the lady wants us to have a little privacy, so you all want to go find a coffee shop or something to entertain yourselves with?'

A small mousey man steps closer and starts to whisper in his ear, but he maintains eye contact with me and brushes away whatever the man is saying.

'No, I've been told she's the best so let's go with it.'

I don't know if he's being genuine or he hopes this blatant flattery will calm me down, but I don't care; I'm too focused on the job at hand to care.

'Your hair and make-up look fine to me, and I do my own styling,' I tell him dismissively, and his group file away as he starts to flick through the suits that have been sent over.

'So what did you have in mind?' he asks, holding up a light grey suit against his body. It would look stunning, he automatically knows what would suit him, but it's not what I had envisaged.

'I was thinking of something more ... dishevelled,' I tell him, taking the suit from him and putting it back on the rail. I lead him through to the back of my studio, to where the bed is.

'Why Miss, I'm really not that kind of boy,' he jokes, and now I laugh too; he's finally put the phone away and it seems the bed has got his attention.

'That's not what I've heard.' I laugh. 'And I thought we could shoot something based on that reputation.'

For a moment he stops, obviously considering it, making me realise he's not as dumb as the media have made out. 'My people wouldn't like it,' he tells me, but that's not a no.

'And what about you?'

'Let's see how it goes.'

'OK. So how about barefoot and shirt unbuttoned for

the first shot, lying on the bed like you've just got in from a long night out?' I ask, checking my cameras are set up properly as he slips off his shoes and socks and quickly poses on the bed.

He follows directions well, and I'm all professionalism behind the camera, judging the best way for him to move and altering the lights accordingly, trying to forget what I want to do next, ignore who exactly it is I have lying on a bed in front of me.

Ignore the heat pulsing between my legs.

It doesn't help that now he only has me to look at I can feel his eyes upon me. Today I'm not in a T-shirt and combats; instead, I've dressed for the occasion in a fitted white shirt and black pencil skirt, aiming for the sexy secretarial look.

The way I feel his eyes undressing me I can tell he appreciates the look.

Which is good, as next I ask him, 'Could you open your shirt?'

He raises an eyebrow, sexily maintaining eye contact as he slowly unbuttons his shirt.

I hide behind my camera. I'm wet already and want him so much, but I know I need to focus a little longer at least.

His chest is more toned than it seemed in his younger shots; he's more muscular, more manly, with a light covering of chest hair. Those younger shots seemed to make him out to be more boy-band material. Now he seems more masculine, less refined and more sexual.

I like it.

When he smiles I realise I'm blushing, my thoughts written across my face as easy to read as saying them aloud.

I turn away, pretending I'm adjusting something on my

camera as I ask, 'How about losing the shirt and trousers?'

He pulls off his shirt completely, then starts to open his jeans before stopping and saying, 'I don't have underwear on.'

I want to laugh; neither do I today.

Instead I tell him, 'The sheet's there to protect your modesty.'

I keep my back turned until I hear the moving and rustling stop, and then I turn back, my heart in my mouth.

I don't know if my pulse is beating harder in my chest or between my legs.

He's naked, the duvet thrown casually across him, as if this were some lazy Sunday morning in bed, not a high-profile photo shoot.

He smiles at me, and I shoot off some pictures quickly, hiding behind my camera once more.

Then I don't want to hide any more.

'How do you feel about making this a little more risqué?'

'What did you have in mind?' he asks, sitting up slightly, the sheet slipping down his toned abs, making my pulse quicken.

'Handcuffs,' I tell him, fetching them out of my bag of props. He looks hesitant. 'If you want to?'

'How can I resist an offer like that from such a sexy lady?' he laughs, but still looks apprehensive as I fasten his left wrist to the headboard. 'Do I need a safe word?'

'Do you think you need one?' I ask, leaning over him, my breasts barely inches from his face as I fasten his right wrist just as quickly.

'No,' he says, moving slightly to get closer.

I pause for a moment, letting him brush his lips against me, then move away, watching as he pulls lightly at his restraints.

'Anyone would think you're trying to take advantage of me,' he laughs.

'I'm just trying to photograph you in a different way,' I tell him, stepping back behind my camera and rattling off a few shots. 'If I were going to take advantage of you, then maybe I'd do something like this ...'

I walk back to the bed and, facing the foot of the bed, straddle him. I push the sheet down, and slowly lean forward and lick his hard cock. He sighs, and I know he can see straight up my skirt, that I'm naked beneath my skirt, must be able to see how wet I am for him.

I wriggle my hips, and my skirt is so tight that it quickly rides up, fully exposing my nakedness for him to see.

'If I wasn't tied up right now,' he starts, then says nothing as I move back and he uses his mouth on me.

He has a talented tongue, and as I lick at his slippery cock and then take it in my mouth it's hard to maintain a rhythm, hard to focus on what he likes as his tongue laps at my clit, driving me wild. It's hard to believe I have one of the most desirable men in the world handcuffed to my bed and licking at my cunt, even as the pressure builds, even as I suck at him harder and faster as my orgasm takes me over.

He groans as I stop sucking at him and climb off the bed.

'Hey, what about me?'

'What about you?' I say, pulling up the sheet to make him look decent once more as I pick up my camera.

He looks pissed off but also amused and confused, and overwhelmingly sexy. He looks horny and frustrated and full of sensuality.

The pictures are amazing.

I want to fuck him so badly. I know it's a bad idea, that the more I do the more chance there is I'm wrecking a career I love so much, but the fact that I shouldn't be doing this just makes it even more appealing.

'You want some too?' I ask, reaching in my bag now for a condom before I change my mind.

His eyes light up, and he looks so perfect I almost wish I hadn't put down the camera.

Almost.

I quickly put the condom on and climb on top of him. He slides inside me easily; I'm wet and slick and ready for him, and start moving immediately, my hips moving in the rhythm I need. He moans in enjoyment, his hands pulling against the cuffs and I know that if his hands were free right now he'd be grabbing me to move the way he wanted. But he can't; I'm in control now, and I like it.

I lean forward to kiss him, tasting myself on him, his tongue meeting mine for the first time, sending a charge of electricity through me. I grind against him, moving slowly and feeling him deep inside me, and though he moves his hips, tries to make me speed up, I take my time, rubbing my body against his, kissing him hard and sighing as I come hard once again.

This time when I move away from the bed he lets loose with a stream of expletives.

'Temper temper,' I laugh, picking up my camera once more, taking some photos I know I'd need to edit later, his cock still on display, but looking so hot and angry and aroused I don't want to stop right now.

'Please, I feel like I'm about to explode,' he moans.

'You're left-handed, yes?'

'Yes,' he replies, obviously confused.

I unlock the handcuff on his left wrist, then dance out of the way quickly before he can grab me.

'There we go then, if you're that desperate.'

He laughs. 'You're seriously unfair, I've made you come twice and you won't even make me come once?'

'Nope,' I tell him. 'But maybe I could give you some encouragement.'

His eyes widen as I slowly undo my shirt, showing off the black and red bra underneath, low cut so my breasts are almost spilling out.

His eyes widen, fixed on my breasts, his hand almost unconsciously going toward his dick.

I pull my skirt up again, showing him my wet cunt, showing him how turned on he makes me, then as I slowly start to tease myself, his hand finally grips his cock hard.

I watch him stroking his cock, hesitantly at first, then more rapidly, eyes going from my face, to my almost exposed breasts, to my fingers stroking my clit.

He watches me as I get closer once more, as I start sighing, my other hand going to my breasts, playing with my nipples through the flimsy material of my bra.

It's too much, and he cries out, jerking on the bed, his cock spurting thick come all over his toned abs. I come too, this last orgasm more intense than the others, leaving me trembling all over.

I throw him the handcuff key and quickly head to the back room, scared of what happens next.

When I return I'm in my combats and old T-shirt, and he is fully dressed. He laughs at my change of outfit.

'You think that would put me off?' he asks, moving closer to me, backing me up against the wall then pinning me against it to kiss me hard.

I melt beneath his touch, flooded with desire for him again, even though I've climaxed more times than I thought I could so quickly.

He moves away, leaving me clinging to the wall for support, my legs weak.

'I'd like to call you sometime.'

'I'm sure your people have my card.'

'That's not quite what I meant.'

'I don't date my subjects.'

'You just fuck them?'

I blush.

'Not usually.'

'I'll call you,' he says, kissing me again.

He does call me, but I find it easier to stick to my principles when I'm not seeing him face to face. We flirt, but we don't meet, and I try to forget about that mad night that should have never happened.

It makes it harder that the photos are so popular.

They're replicated everywhere, praised for bringing out his raw sensuality, for their sexiness, their *edge*.

The photos I don't publish could earn me a fortune, but they're for me, for my private collection.

Without them I could believe that night was pure fantasy.

With them I believe that the fantasy could happen again.

Have Your Cake and Eat It
by Jeremy Smith

The kids had gone, leaving a mess of balloons and plates; all that was left to do was clean up the village hall before the W.I. turned up. I enjoyed catering but it was always a bit annoying to see so much food go to waste, maybe jelly and custard were out of fashion, replaced by healthy carrots and celery.

Leigh, my boyfriend, scurried by with another bag of rubbish, he was helping me tidy up so we could get back quicker, he didn't need to say why, but I knew. The big giveaway was the bulge in his tight jeans that had been getting bigger all afternoon. Not that I minded, the sight of it turned me on, it gave me a warm feeling just below my stomach, the one you get when you know that someone is lusting after you. He'd been away working for a week so I knew he was going to be really desperate for it, nearly as much as I was. In fact, I couldn't wait to feel him slide his hard shaft in me and I had taken any excuse I could to accidentally rub against it when I passed him just to see if I could make it bigger. He knew I was teasing him and loved every second of it.

In some ways it was good when he was away because it gave him time to fantasise about me and he'd get so worked up he'd come back with the kinkiest of suggestions. I'd been tied up, spanked, we had set up the camcorder and watched ourselves have live sex. One time we even went online so all the world could watch, and by the amount of comments we got I think that most of the world did. A threesome was one I had yet to build up the courage to do, I had thought about it enough and with both sexes. Of course Leigh wanted two women and although it would be exciting to explore another woman's body, there was something about having two cocks that sort of fascinated me.

The sex on the beach had been great, and the time we joined the mile-high club in that airplane toilet had been quite acrobatic.

Leigh certainly liked his kinks.

One of my favourites was changing room sex, I would take some clothes into a shop cubicle and he would follow and pull the curtain across. To know there was only that thin material between us and the outside world was such a turn on and of course you couldn't make a sound in case you were heard. I would bend over for him and he would just lift my skirt up and pull down my knickers and he'd be inside me like a chased rabbit down a hole. Hard, fast and fantastic and we would be back outside before his come had finished trickling out of me. I smiled and wondered what little depraved fantasy he had lined up for me this time.

I hurriedly started to gather up the bowls of food, a bit too quick and spilt some strawberry drink over my blouse – that stain wouldn't come out unless it was soaked – so I started to unbutton my top when Leigh came in.

'You starting without me, Julie?' He smiled hopefully.

'No. I spilt some drink on it,' I took my blouse off revealing my white lace bra, of course his eyes looked straight at my breasts as they jiggled above the cups.

'There's some juice on your neck.' Leigh bent in closer, lowered his face and gently sucked up the drips.

His breath was warm and his tongue moist, a shiver went down my back and my nipples erupted against the tight lace material. God it felt so good, especially after a week's separation.

His hand moved to my bra and he gave me a testing squeeze, I pushed my nipple against his palm.

'You like it when I nibble your neck then?'

'Mmmm,' was all I could answer.

He dangled his fingers in the juice pitcher and sprinkled some more onto me. Again his mouth followed the drips, this time along my shoulder. He pushed his hips against my thigh and rolled the hardness of his cock against it.

'So is it just juice you like dripped on you?'

'As long as you lick it off I don't care.'

'In that case!' He reached for a jug of custard.

Before I knew what had happened he had put a dollop of custard into my cleavage and began to lick it out, burying his face between my tits as he squeezed them together, snaring his nose. To feel his tongue flick against my body was sending shivers all over me. I wondered how much custard he had. I undid my skirt and let it fall to the floor. I needed him to lick more than my cleavage.

It took a moment for him to realise that I was standing before him in just my bra and panties, but when he caught site of the tight material stretching over the mound between my legs his smile widened.

'What's going on here?' he said.

'You have the custard, you tell me.' I smiled back at him wickedly.

He ran a finger down my stomach and onto my panties, I held my breath as he traced it along my furrow making me squirm, making me want him even more.

'You're so wet,' he said. 'Anybody would think

you've been having dirty thoughts.'

'The same ones you're having.' I pushed my breasts out towards him. 'Get me sticky,' I demanded.

He didn't need telling twice. He raised the custard jug, pulled open one of my bra cups and filled it with the creamy yellow liquid then let it snap back onto me. I gave a sharp intake of breath, the custard was cold as it squidged out over my tit. He took it in his hand and gave it a rub, custard oozed out through the lace as his hand drew over it. He opened up my other cup and filled that one, then squashed that on to me, cold and wet he rubbed it.

'How does that feel?' he asked, still massaging.

'It feels ... nice ... dirty. I like it.'

'Good, because I haven't finished yet,' he said as his cock throbbed eagerly at me through his jeans. 'Take your bra off.'

I undid the clasp at the back and even with the straps off my bra was stuck to me. I slowly peeled it down, the custard trying to suck it back to my skin. He prised it off over my nipples and threw it onto one of the tables. My breasts bounced free before him impatiently heaving for more attention, although already coated he poured more on, smearing it over with his hand, drips flicking from my hard bullets, it felt a bit like when you spread cold after-sun on but more so, sweeter. My tits slipped in and out of his hand as if trying to escape and when he caught them, flesh and custard moulded between his fingers. Drips fell on to my stomach and he bobbed down to angel kiss them off. He dripped more on me and it felt divine, each spot a cold teasing sensation sending my muscles into spasm.

He took a teaspoon and filled it, then he flicked it at me splashing it over my stomach, the coolness tensing my muscles. I imagined it was his spunk spraying on me.

'Undo my trousers,' he commanded. 'Get my cock out.'

I reached out, yanked at his zip, he wiggled as I pulled down and he kicked his jeans to one side of the hall. His dark boxers were already stained with a silvered trail of pre-come, his cock jutted forward trying to push through the material. I knew my own knickers were just as damp.

'You gonna fuck me now?' I asked, still thinking about his spunk.

'Oh no. Playtime isn't over.' He grinned as he stared at my tits. 'On your knees.'

I obediently knelt down.

'Squash your tits together.'

I put a hand either side of them and pushed, my cleavage became deep enough to get lost in. Leigh reached for the custard again and poured it down the dark valley, then he manoeuvred himself in front of me, and slid his cock straight between my sticky mounds. His coated yellow knob appeared between them, slowly he pumped away at my chest and I tightened my flesh around him. Each time his cockhead appeared I dabbed it with my tongue licking it clean of its now sugary pre-come.

'God that feels good,' he sighed, sliding his whole length in and out. 'It's almost as slippery as your pussy.'

He had such a look of contentment on his face that I wondered if he was going to come there and then and splash his load over my neck and chin. I opened my mouth, half expecting to catch his salty jism but instead he slipped out. His hand snaked between my legs and touched my swollen pussy, testing the waters.

'Your knickers are soaking,' he said. 'And you're so hot.'

'I really need a fuck,' I half pleaded.

'Better cool you down a bit first.' He took a plate of

jelly from the table and with one hand he pulled open my waist band, with the other he grabbed a fist full of jelly, his hand shot into my knickers and cupping between my legs he pushed it onto me making me squeal. If I'd thought the custard was cold this was something else. He slowly circled his palm against me, smearing the sticky coldness over and between my lips. Goose pimples erupted over my body and as he slipped a sneaky finger inside me, I squealed again.

He pulled his finger out and sucked it.

'Mmm, you taste of strawberries,' he said and then emptied the rest of the plate into my knickers. It was so cold against my burning heat I half expected to see steam as the melting lumps were held tight against me by my damp lace.

'Walk about,' he said.

I stood up, my knickers bulging with jelly, a small run of it trickled, ice-cold, down my thigh. I moved some more and let it squelch around between my legs. I bent over to show him my arse and it squelched up into my hole, cold and tingly.

'You're enjoying that, aren't you?' he murmured.

'More than you know.' I shivered and rubbed my hand between my legs pushing it tight to my clit.

I saw another jelly on the table, complete out of the mould. I took it on the dish over to Leigh and I pushed two fingers deep into it making a scarlet slit in its wobbly surface.

'Your turn,' I said. He looked at me puzzled for a moment. 'Fuck this.' I grinned at him.

For a moment he just stood there, then he took his cock in his hand and with the jelly held at thigh level he slowly guided it into the hole I'd made. I could see it slide in through transparent sides, his foreskin pulling on and off as he fucked it.

'Oh. That's freezing!' His eyes widened.

He pushed himself in and out of the cold pussy I'd made. Each time it slurped and sucked, wobbling the whole plate. His thrusts make my tits wobble in time with it. His balls slapped against the smooth surface, contracting against the cold shock but if anything his cock got bigger. I can't explain why, but watching him fuck the jelly really aroused me. Given the chance I think he would have kept going, but under his onslaught it started to disintegrate.

We were both into this new kink now and looked around for some other depraved way to use the food.

'Chocolate gateaux,' he said. 'I'm going to eat it.'

'How is that kinky?'

'Well, Julie, I'm going to eat it off your pussy.'

He walked to another table, his pendulous cock swinging in front of him, when he returned he put the cake on the floor. I looked down at it covered in cream with cherries on top.

'Take your knickers off, squat down and sit on it,' he said.

My undies now felt like they were glued to me, stuck firm by the jelly but with a gentle tug and a wiggle they slid down my legs and puddled at my feet. I kicked them away and they flew through the air, slapped against a window and stuck to it.

I stood astride the cake and lined myself up. Slowly I lowered myself down. When I hit, it was like sitting on cool mud. I sank in and felt the cream work its way up my bum cleavage, as it pressed at my holes my arse puckered against the chill. I started to sway my hips, grinding myself down into it, squashing it into a chocolaty mess between my thighs. It felt so good, so dirty. I thought about climaxing as he watched me get off on this cake, watching my cunt messier than I thought possible. This sex really was dirty.

I put my hands behind me on the floor and raised my stomach, with my legs wide apart I presented him with the chocolate delight.

'Eat me out then,' I told him.

He got on all fours and his face fell onto my sex. Greedily he licked and ate, letting his tongue clean out every hole and fold of skin, he buried himself into me flicking at my clit sending shivers down my neck and along my back. He kept licking even when the cake had gone, pushing his tongue deep inside me. The cake must have been good but I knew he liked my juices better and right now it was dripping from me.

I looked down my food-streaked body, the custard on my tits, the jelly and cake that clung to my pubes, and then I looked at his face still between my legs as he ate away and I just had to have more of this messy sex. I wanted to have the stickiest most slippery fuck possible. I let him lick me for a while longer, feeling the energy build up in my stomach, my muscles began to tighten as my orgasm started to grow, but I was just teasing myself, I wasn't going to let myself come yet, I wanted this one to be a screamer. I moved away from him and then pushed him down.

'Lie on your back,' I said.

He lay flat, all apart from his manhood that flexed in the air. I grabbed a handful of custard and slapped it onto his cock, watching it slide down his thick veined shaft. Slowly I started to wank him, working the custard all over, rubbing it over his exposed knob, a dribble of pre-come mixed in. I grabbed another dollop and splashed it onto his balls, and rubbed them as I wanked. He arched his back and pushed himself into my fist, groaning. I knew he wanted me to go faster but I kept it slow, I was going to bring him to the boil gently. This had to get far messier before I would let him climax. I eased his foreskin up and down, stretching it tight then back over his knob. his groans increased each time. Then I released his balls and started to give him a double hander, twisting each hand in opposite directions as they went up and down. I could almost see his balls grow heavy as he readied his load.

'Not yet, Leigh,' I whispered.

I reached out for the custard jug and tipped most of it over his cock and stomach. Then I straddled him and lowered myself down, he watched as the pussy he had just freshly cleaned descended onto him, and his cock lay flat underneath me.

'What're you doing now?' he asked.

'I'm going to rub my pussy all over you.' Slowly I eased my way forward, feeling his cock slide between my pouting lips. A wave of custard pushed along with me, over his stomach and up to his chest, my pussy leaving a trail behind it. I swayed my hips backwards and forwards, dragging my clit along him, teasing it against the rough hairs of his chest. I slipped and slid all over, getting messier and messier. I moved back down to his cock, letting his knob just ease its way to my hot entrance and then I pulled away. I lowered myself onto him further down his shaft, and slowly masturbated myself against his throbbing hardness as he flexed and bucked against me. I was so near to coming, but I didn't want this feeling to end.

I grabbed for the rest of the jelly on the plate and dropped it on his chest. I lowered my chest down and rubbed my tits into it, my achingly stiff nips massaging against his. I took hold of one breast and squashed it forward for him, red jelly stuck to it ready for him to lick away. I offered it to his mouth and he sucked me inside, stretching my nipple out. He clamped his teeth around it, sending a sharp exquisite spark all the way through me. Then, still held between his teeth, he flicked the end of it with his tongue. He released me and looked at my other tit. I held it tight in my hand and pushed it into his face, jelly smeared across his cheek and chin before he opened his mouth and clamped down on me. God that felt good.

'Suck it,' I sighed. I was pulled in deeper, feeling the blood rush to the skin. He nipped at me.

'Bite it.' His teeth chewed painfully on me, almost more than I could bear. 'Harder.' I squealed with delight and rubbed my cunt against him, squashing my puffy mound hard onto his cock. I pushed more tit into his mouth, and with my free hand I reached behind me and fondled his custard-sticky balls.

'I'm going to fuck you so hard,' he said.

'You'd better.'

'I'm going to stretch that pretty little cunt of yours wide open.'

'Yes, yes.' I rubbed against him harder, feeling his cockhead edge towards my opening. I sat up on him and his hands reached for my breasts, pulling at them, tweaking my already red nipples, stretching them out and pinching them.

'Say you want me to fuck you, Julie.'

'Fuck me, fuck me hard,' I panted.

'On your knees and bend over. Let's do this properly.'

Hurriedly I dismounted him, got on all fours and with my head on the floor I stuck my arse high in the air, my puffy lips pushed out from between my thighs already open and inviting as I moved my knees further apart.

'You look so sexy,' he whispered. 'Just one more thing to finish the picture.'

The next moment, instead of feeling his cock push into me, I felt more custard being poured at the top of my arse cleavage, it slowly flowed south over my arse hole and down to my pussy, for a moment it seemed to linger there then I could see it drip off and puddle on the floor. I saw Leigh's face lower towards me, and starting at my pussy hole he licked all the way back up my cleft, and over my arse until he had licked and cleaned the whole channel. With his tongue gliding over both my holes I felt like I was going to explode. I pushed myself back onto him in the hope his tongue would go deeper but then he moved and I held my breath for what I had been waiting for.

He eased my legs wider apart and then I felt his cock begin to nudge at me, finding my secret path to my velvety depths. Once at the entrance he leant forward, and pushed his way inside, his thick swollen member widening my passage to accommodate its girth. I moaned loudly as I felt his balls began to slap against my clit as he pounded his way in, faster he went. His hands gripped at my hips, slipping on custard. Deeper he went, I started to feel light headed, my heart pounding as my tits swayed to and fro. I ground myself against him, meeting every thrust. My moans became more like a whimper as I waited. I clenched my fists as the sparks danced in my stomach and then it happened, like an explosion in my mind I came. I yelled out and still he thrust into me, pumping harder and harder, in and out of my sloppy hole, I yelled some more until gradually the feeling began to subside, but I kept the momentum going for him. Leigh began to groan as well, I looked at him over my shoulder, he was biting down on his lip, his eyes closed in concentration. Deep inside me I could feel his cock begin to jerk and buck against my tight muscles. Then, if possible, it began to get stiffer. I reached a hand back between my legs and let his balls rub against my palm and he drove forward, they were hot and heavy, hanging low as they swung.

'That's it, fuck me, stretch me,' I urged him on.

He opened his eyes and looked at me. He mouth fell open as he was about to come and then he pulled out of me, took his juice coated cock in his hand and aimed at my arse. A long stream of come shot out of him, splashing onto my cheeks, then another, this time between them, running down my crack and onto my pussy, then one more. Breathing heavily, he rubbed his cock and one last gush covered me. For a second he looked proudly at the mess he had made and then with a smile he rubbed his come all over my cheeks.

'Perfect,' he said.

'The best,' I replied with a giggle.

From the back of the hall came the voice of a little old lady. 'Don't stop on our account,' it said.

Shocked I looked over as an audience of several elderly women stared at us.

'Would you like some jam on that?' One of them held up a jar in her hand and smiled at us.